"Weren't we working on body language?"

Joe spoke softly and leaned toward Marla. "I have a few things to say on that subject."

His closeness sent her senses spinning. "No, we were discussing power-talk." Her pen clattered to the floor when Joe framed her face with his hands and kissed her, but she managed to say, "Before we get carried away, let's review the delivery techniques."

"Hmm . . . keep your voice even and relaxed." He trailed his hands down her arms. "How can I relax when I'm so close to you?"

"Perhaps you should stand an arm's length away." Marla's heart started beating faster. "What about speed?"

"I should take my time. Long breaths, short sentences." He stroked the wildly pulsating spot at the base of her throat. "I'm breathless at the moment. And a little hot."

Feeling equally breathless, Marla capitulated. "You know, maybe it's high time we had our lesson on body language, after all."

Although **Mary Tate Engels** is a transplanted Southerner—she was born in Chattanooga, Tennessee—she has grown to love the White Mountains of central Arizona. This fondness, as well as her fascination with Apache culture, are evident in *Speak to the Wind*.

Well established in the romance genre, Mary has published sixteen romance novels under the pseudonym Tate McKenna. She has also coauthored six other romances, one of which is a Temptation, written with a partner under the name Corey Keaton.

Mary and her husband live with their three teenage sons in Tucson, Arizona.

Books by Corey Keaton

HARLEQUIN TEMPTATION
194—THE NESTING INSTINCT

Don't miss any of our special offers. Write to us at the following address for information on our newest releases.

Harlequin Reader Service
901 Fuhrmann Blvd., P.O. Box 1397, Buffalo, NY 14240
Canadian address: P.O. Box 603,
Fort Erie, Ont. L2A 5X3

Speak to the Wind

MARY TATE ENGELS

Harlequin Books

TORONTO • NEW YORK • LONDON
AMSTERDAM • PARIS • SYDNEY • HAMBURG
STOCKHOLM • ATHENS • TOKYO • MILAN

To Adalie and Paul, with much love and gratitude for the cabin and inspiration for this book; and for the unlimited love and support through all the years

Published August 1988

ISBN 0-373-25315-X

Prologue

The Ritual

THE ONLY CONTACT Marla Eden had with the outside world was the Apache language radio station.

Before turning the radio on, she rested her hand on top and listened to the absolute quiet around the cabin. The solitude of the mountains spoke to her, filling her again with the necessary ingredients for carrying on her work, her life. That's the way it had been for many years, since she was a child.

Of course, she didn't realize what the mountains did for her then, didn't know of their reviving magic. But now Marla was convinced that when she returned to Phoenix at the end of the week, she'd be rejuvenated. She could once again pursue her life, which was her business.

Speechcraft, the company she had formed three years ago to teach corporate executives better communications skills, had grown rapidly as a result of her constant attention and workaholic practices. Her most popular seminars were Speak Easy into the Microphone and Smile, Rise and Shine, both of which had been conceived right here in this cabin.

Marla clicked on the radio, and static crackled over the airwaves. Sometimes late at night she could pick up an English station from the nearest town of Show Low or even from faraway Flagstaff. Most of the time, though, she tuned in the local station and tolerated its occasional static.

She listened abstractedly, not understanding the Indian words but finding certain pleasure in the rhythm and exotic sound of the Apache language. Marla sipped her cream-laced coffee to the harmony of the world news broadcast in a strange combination of English mingled with Apache. Then the station returned to its regular country music, and she slid into her coat.

Marla's early-morning walks by the lake had become a habit—a glorious, refreshing ritual. She stepped out onto the porch and inhaled the cedar-scented air. The distinctive fragrance was as soothing to her senses as the Apache language.

A wild cry pierced the serenity, and Marla dashed off the porch to search the skies.

There he is! Swooping from his nesting area high in the mountains, surveying his domain. Bold. Flying free. Rare. Bald eagle.

Her heart quickened at the sight, filling her with a combination of admiration and pride. He was truly grand, which was why she'd used him as her logo on her business cards and letterhead along with the inspirational phrase "Rise above the ordinary." He certainly did.

The eagle's arrogant white head thrust toward the sun, his wingspan at least seven feet as he sailed across the orange-streaked dawn sky. Ebony wings whispered against the wind as he banked toward the lake, and Marla hurried along the road so that she could watch his ritual.

Thin fog, filmy as angel's hair, hung low. The lake shimmered silver, reflecting the faint morning light off its flat surface. The slick, mirrored veneer was marred only by a single fishing boat bearing two dark-haired men, huddled against the crisp cold air.

THE BOAT ROCKED as the larger of the two men shifted for a better look at the splendid bird that circled them. "We've got a competitor for the next trout, Uncle Will. A bald. So massive. Do you know how long it's been since I've seen an eagle flying like that? So free."

The older man lifted his bushy gray eyebrows curiously. "Don't they have eagles in California?"

"Not where I live. Too populated."

"Then how do you . . ." He halted, knowing the answer to his question before it was asked. He shook his head and looked away. "I'm afraid you've forgotten all the old ways, Joseph."

"Not forgotten, Uncle Will. Just not practiced."

"Then it's time, high time—" Will's heavily accented words were interrupted by the eagle's feral scream as he buzzed their boat, looking for fish or perhaps a duck.

Joe shielded his eyes and continued to watch the sky, the fishing rod forgotten in his large hands. His voice lowered to a rumble. "Lord, he's magnificent."

"He's a big one, all right. Eats too many fish," Will grumbled, then began fiddling with his fishing line, paying the bird little heed. "It's a sign. A sign that you are welcome here again." He jerked the rod, then patiently reeled in a struggling rainbow trout.

The eagle shrieked as if in protest.

Joe sighed heavily and gazed out over the lake. A sign from the mountain spirits? Did he really believe that? If the truth be known, this same eagle probably came here every morning for his breakfast. Then it wasn't a sign, but a habit. A ritual. A survival technique.

Joe knew he had to change his way of thinking, change it to the Apache way if this was going to work. It wouldn't be easy for a man who'd been gone so long.

He gazed at his uncle, whose burnt-copper hands patiently baited the fishhook again and flicked the line into the water. Joe studied his own hands, also copper but not so worn. Still, they were Apache hands. Maybe he'd been gone too long, had changed too much.

Or maybe—he watched the great bird dive for a fish swimming close to the lake's surface—maybe the eagle *was* a good sign that it was time.

The magnetic bald eagle flew away with his breakfast grasped in curved talons, dark-feathered wings spangled with sunlight. His untamed call of pride lifted to the mountain peaks of central Arizona, home of the wind and of the mountain spirits.

1

MARLA EDEN'S APPEARANCE in the Apache reservation grocery store often garnered attention from the native Americans gathered there. It was more than her attractiveness, more than her tawny blond hair and chestnut-brown eyes. She had a casual self-confidence that invited women to exchange greetings with her and men to offer to carry out her groceries. There was no reason to expect today would be any different, but when she stepped inside Berg's Post, no one looked her way.

A small group clustered around someone seated in the back of the store beyond the stack of Pendleton blankets. The voice was masculine, pleasant and low toned. Because of her interest in public speaking, it was a sound Marla couldn't ignore.

Listening with growing curiosity, she picked out her supplies. When they were assembled on the counter next to the old-fashioned cash register, she glanced around for the checker. No one came to her service, so she moved toward the assembly in the rear.

"Excuse me. Can someone check me out?"

The group parted for a young woman who hurried toward Marla with an apologetic smile. "Sorry."

For a moment the Indians stared at Marla.

For a moment she stared back, not at them, but at the man seated in the center of their circle. He was Apache, though distinctive from those around him. Dressed in beige cords and an ecru turtleneck sweater, he was a large, broad-shouldered man whose presence dominated the group. His ebony gaze met hers, locked and stared steadily as if able for that brief moment to see inside her soul. Then the Indians congregated around the speaker again, and she lost sight of him.

But she couldn't dismiss the feeling that contact with the man gave her. It wasn't the usual male's curious stare or the straightforward admiration she sometimes received. There was something singularly compelling about this man.

Marla turned to the sloe-eyed girl behind the counter and tried to steer her attention to the store owner's whereabouts. "Isn't Mrs. Berg here today?"

"She went into town to see the doctor."

"Is she ill?"

"Her arthritis is acting up again."

"Tell her Marla was here, will you? And that I hope she's feeling better soon." Marla counted out the cash for her purchases. "Tell her I'll stop by to see her before I leave."

Cradling her bag of groceries in one arm, Marla glanced back at the dark-haired assembly, subconsciously seeking another look at the mysterious man whose eyes did strange things to her. But he was hidden. She could hear him speaking, hear his audience commenting, hear him responding in his low, even-toned voice. She wanted to step closer, to know what he had to say that interested them so completely. But she wasn't included and to join them would have been rude.

Marla drove away from the little settlement still wondering about the man and what attraction he had for the people gathered around him. She liked the gentle way he spoke to them and admired that natural ability to mesmerize a crowd. He had mesmerized her, too, in the brief moment when their eyes had met.

As the road wound upward into the heart of the White Mountains, Marla was again filled with a growing exhilaration, a sensation that was still somewhat of a mystery to her. She eased back on the accelerator, reminding herself that she was in no hurry. This wasn't the fast lane; this was her escape to the mountains, to the cabin and its memories. She forgot about the Apache with the sonorous voice and the bewitching eyes.

The thirty-minute journey to her cabin was like a step back in time, taking the traveler from air-polluted civilization to the frontierlike High Meadow Apache Reservation in the heart of the White Mountains. And Marla loved it.

Pulling into the familiar driveway, she paused to listen to the wind whispering in the pines and to inhale the fresh, cedar-scented air. Grabbing her groceries, she mounted the porch steps and intruded on the strong silence of the rooms. The floor creaked as she headed for the kitchen and began storing her cans.

Memories dominated the place. Everything seemed to ignite still-vivid recollections of her father. He had built the place when she and her brother, Rob, were young. It was exciting to have a cabin located on the Apache Indian reservation where the fields and woods provided wilderness settings for their childish games.

Their parents, along with several Phoenix friends, had signed long-term land leases with the High Meadow Apaches and built a cabin on the lake. The place had become a refuge from the stifling summer heat and a snow-covered winter playground for the Richey family.

"Everyone will benefit," her father had reasoned. "We want the vacation spot and are willing to pay for it. The Apaches want the rent. It makes for good business and good relations between the two cultures."

Marla had never questioned his wisdom. Still didn't. She knew how much fun it was to vacation in the White Mountains and believed him to be right. Her parents even talked of retiring here. But Alan Richey had died of a sudden heart attack long before retirement age.

The cabin remained as a tribute of Alan's love for his family. Over the past four years since his untimely death they had all enjoyed it. Now, though, only Marla came to the mountains. Their mother, Francine, was too busy with a new career in real estate and a social life that included a suitor. Rob's wife got carsick traveling the winding mountain roads, so they seldom came.

Marla was grateful for this gift from her father, especially now. It gave her a quiet thinking place. On many of her long walks by the lake she was thrilled by the wildlife—deer, rabbits, occasionally elk. Red-tailed hawks frequently circled above the pine tops, and occasionally she'd sight one of the rare bald eagles that lived in the ponderosa forests. Late at night Marla could hear the yip-yip of roaming coyotes or the plaintive cry of a prowling cougar.

Usually it took her about twenty-four hours to unwind after arriving. Then, because she couldn't stay away from it any longer, Marla would start thinking about work, just a little. Tonight she rekindled the fire and took her supper into the living room to eat in front of the huge stone fireplace that covered one wall. Dipping crispy corn chips into warmed-up canned chili, she studied the layout for a new business brochure. Occasionally she'd stop to stoke the fire or fix another cup of spiced cider.

She heard the coyotes, then another noise—like the slamming of a car door—drew her attention. Marla sat very still, listening. The coyotes hushed. She heard footsteps in the gravel driveway, then boots clattered on the wooden front porch.

She glanced at the clock on the mantel. Nearly ten. Who would be in this area at this hour? When she heard a knock, Marla rose and put her ear to the solid oak door. With a forced calmness she called, "Who's there?"

A man answered, but his voice was muffled. She heard, "...car trouble...have a phone...make a call..."

Although she couldn't hear it clearly, something about the voice was familiar, something compelling and reassuring. Marla opened the door a small crack and peered out. The stranger on her porch loomed dark and bold and massive shouldered. An Indian, she quickly decided. A closer look revealed deep brown eyes that she'd seen before, intense eyes that could almost see inside your soul. He was the man who had held the Apaches' interest in Berg's Post.

She opened the door wider, and a gust of cold air rushed inside. Even though it was only September, night temperatures approached freezing. "What's your name again?"

His intense ebony eyes flickered recognition as she became visible. Their slightly almond shape hinted of distant Oriental ancestry as he squinted at the light in her room. His angular face was shadowed and intriguing; his lips were open but not quite smiling. Exotic coppery skin took on a mahogany glow from the firelight. "Joseph Quintero."

Quintero, she thought. The name sounded familiar, but she'd never met this man, just seen him in the store.

"Sorry to bother you at this late hour," he said in a low, pleasant tone. "But my car's stalled by the lake. Actually, it's my cousin's car. Maybe you know him. John Yates?" He gestured toward the dirt road that edged High Meadow Lake.

"Yates?" Marla shook her head. "I don't think so."

"Look, I know it's late and this is inconvenient, but if you'd just make a call for me, I'd appreciate it." His warm breath vaporized in the cold air and dark eyes darted past her shoulder to the blazing fireplace.

Marla evaluated the situation and decided she could trust him. "Why don't you come on in and use the phone yourself? It's freezing cold out there."

"You're sure you don't mind?"

She stepped back to admit him. "Come on."

They both knew the Indian community was on the other side of the lake, a good three miles away. This side, where Marla lived, was inhabited mostly by non-Indian families, people like her who came up for vacations. Part of its appeal was that the area was basically crime free. Anyway, in remote areas like this, people helped each other out of jams.

He eased into the warm living room, taking up a fair amount of space with his bulk. "You were the one in Berg's Post today, weren't you?"

"Yes." She felt surprised but pleased that he remembered her from that fleeting glance. "And you were there holding court."

He shrugged and his large shoulders moved inside his gray brushed twill jacket. "Not really. Just talking." The meeting had been much more than that, though, and Joe was still considering the problems discussed by the concerned group.

His compelling gaze again captured hers until she broke the contact by moving to shut the door. Marla tried to remain calm in this man's presence. But she felt his power and his masculine attraction. She hadn't been so affected by a man in years.

He rubbed his ungloved hands together briskly. "I would shake hands, but these mitts are like ice."

"I'm Marla Eden. Nice to meet you, Joseph." She extended her hand. "And I'm used to cold hands." Her business training stressed the importance of shaking hands, of establishing equality. The gesture sometimes bridged gaps between strangers.

The big man reached out, his large hand engulfing hers. "Joe. Call me Joe; everybody does. I'm glad you're home. Yours is the only house with a light on in this whole stretch of road, so I had quite a walk ahead."

For a man with cold hands, Joe Quintero emitted a certain warmth that radiated from his palm to hers, then rushed throughout her body. His hand was large, his grip strong. The man also possessed a hefty natural dose of charisma. Something special.

When he released her hand, Marla felt a jolt of emptiness. She told herself it was relief. "Your name sounds familiar, Joe. Any relation to Will Quintero?" She knew Will Quintero as a member of the Apache Tribal Council who had been in charge of collecting rent on the cabin's land lease for many years.

Joe smiled and his eyes crinkled warmly at the corners. "Will's my uncle. I hoped you'd recognize my last name. Figured if you had spent any time around here you would."

"I've been coming here since I was a child." She pushed her blond hair behind one ear, then pointed to the kitchen. "The phone's in there."

With a grace surprising in a man so large he moved into the kitchen and picked up the phone receiver.

Marla stood by the fireplace sipping her cider and trying not to eavesdrop on his conversation. But she couldn't help listening. It was simple and to the point. He had such a nice masculine resonance to his tone; she liked listening to him. She noted that he didn't have the usual accent of most of the

Indians in the area. It was part of her business to notice those things.

He walked back into the living room, rubbing his hands together. "Thanks. My rescue party is on the way."

"Do they live far?"

"A few miles away." He took her measure in the flickering firelight. She looked thin in stone-washed Levi's and a baggy purple sweater. He liked the way she wore her blond, shoulder-length hair, casually parted on one side. Instinctively his eyes went to her hands, which were wrapped around a heavy pottery mug. A simple gold band circled the ring finger on her right hand. It looked like a wedding band, but it was on the wrong hand. He could only assume she wasn't married, for there was no ring on her left.

She reminded him of a delicate, fragile crystal goblet of champagne. He couldn't take his eyes off her and felt slightly intoxicated with her beauty. She carried herself well, with confidence. But there was something about her expression, her darkly serious eyes, that issued vulnerability, perhaps even pain. And Joe was immediately curious about her.

Her down-to-earth beauty appealed to him. She was refreshing and lively, not entirely innocent. Her hair framed her oval face like strands of silk. The firelight seemed to turn it golden, and he flexed his large hands to quell the urge to touch it.

Flexing didn't help much, so Joe stuffed his hands into his pockets and leaned against the doorframe, trying to appear casual. "You say you've been coming to the mountains since you were a child? Are you here vacationing with your family?"

"No, I . . ." Maria hesitated to tell him she was alone. "I'm taking a few days off from work."

"Then you must be from Phoenix or Tucson."

"Phoenix." Marla lifted the mug to her lips, then lowered it before taking a drink. "Excuse me for not asking sooner. Would you like something hot to drink? I'm having cider, but I could fix you coffee."

He gave her a grateful smile. "Cider sounds fine."

She edged past him on her way into the kitchen, and he caught a whiff of her delicate floral perfume. In that split second Joe thought of wildflowers on a hillside, of sprinkling them over her, over her bare skin. And he wanted to bury his face in her hair, to inhale her sweetness. Struggling with his willpower, Joe turned in the doorway so that they could continue to talk. "Where do you work, Marla?"

"I travel quite a bit making presentations, but my home base is Phoenix."

"What kind of presentations do you make?"

"I'm a business communications consultant, and the presentations usually contain an overall view of my firm."

"Okay," he conceded, folding his arms across his expansive chest. "What do communications consultants do?"

"Among other things, we teach people how to speak in public."

He looked at her curiously. "How to make speeches, huh?"

With a little smile she gave him her well-rehearsed business spiel. "At Speechcraft we instruct our clients in all phases of verbal and nonverbal communication techniques, including body language, written memos and reports and media events. We specialize in public speaking with ease and confidence."

"Sounds impressive. You mean you can teach someone how to conduct a news conference?"

"Of course. There are learnable skills to that, just as in any other craft." She reached up for another clay mug. "Politicians, or political candidates, frequently take our courses, especially now with so much news media emphasis."

"Oh?" His eyebrows shot up at the word "politicians." But she couldn't possibly know about his intentions. It was still a carefully guarded secret.

She poured steaming cider into the mug and handed it to him. "Here you go. We can wait by the fireplace."

"Thanks. This smells great." He followed her into the living room and took a seat in the chair opposite her. "I haven't had cider in ages."

"I only drink it when I come up here. Maybe it's the chilly air or the atmosphere that invites curling up by the fire with a cup of something hot in your hands."

"How often do you come up?"

"Never often enough. Usually two or three times a year."

"Well, that's more often than I make it."

Marla cocked her head. "Then you don't live around here?"

"No, I'm from California." Joe gazed at her with a straightforward, unreadable expression.

"I just assumed you lived here." She felt foolish. She knew all Indians didn't live on reservations. Her assumptions about this man were all wrong so far and piqued her curiosity even more.

Joe picked up a Speechcraft brochure she'd left on the table and scanned it. His thumb pointed out the majestic bald eagle drawing and slogan imprinted on the front. "Is that what you do, Marla? Teach people to rise above the ordinary?"

"I give them the tools. After that it's up to the individual." She paused with a modest little laugh. "You can see my High Meadow Lake influence. Can't help it, I guess. There's a huge bald eagle that feeds at the lake almost every morning. It's a ritual, like clockwork. I watch him and think he's absolutely grand. He definitely rises above the ordinary, even among eagles."

Joe dropped the brochure to his knee and gazed strangely at her. "I've seen him. Early this morning, in fact. Uncle Will and I were fishing."

"You were in that boat on the lake?"

He nodded. "Where were you?"

"I took a walk."

For a few silent seconds, a silken moment in time, they realized they had shared the morning, both the magnificent sight of the eagle's ritual and the awesome feeling that they had been privileged observers.

Finally Marla spoke, her tone hushed. "I often take a walk early in the morning when it's quiet. It's a good time to think."

She halted clumsily, feeling she was rapidly losing her composure in this simple conversation with a stranger. Yet she knew instinctively that there was no such thing as simple conversation with this intriguing man sitting across from her. She took a deep breath, fighting to remain at ease, to put into action the skills she taught.

"You're right," he agreed quietly. "It's a special place, especially for those who appreciate it." He paused, then deftly changed the subject. "I'm curious about what kind of clients you have, Marla."

Marla launched into the comfortable territory of Speechcraft. "The seminars we do for corporations usually deal with basic communications skills and include business-related information. We also work with clients who've been suddenly thrown into a public situation and want a little help, especially in dealing with the media. Or those heading in that direction who want the skills before they get there. My most recent clients were a group of rock stars."

"Are you kidding? Who?"

"Privileged information." She gave her head a quick shake. "They rose to stardom too rapidly to adjust to their popularity. We should all have their problem, right? These kids had no concept how instant stardom would affect their lives. Suddenly they couldn't do anything without the world knowing."

"So what was your advice?"

"Of course they didn't need to learn public speaking per se. We worked on retaining some degree of privacy while keeping the fans and press happy. Fame and fortune aren't always as wonderful as they appear on the surface. There are lots of demands."

"I never stopped to consider it might be a problem." He drained his mug and set it down on the table. "Just curious. How did you manage all this without the press knowing about it?"

She smiled coyly. "It's our business to be completely confidential. Most of our individual clients demand anonymity. In this case, I spent several weeks on the road with them and no one knew who I was. There are so many groupies, so it was easy to include me. It isn't as easy if the client is a politician with a family. Recently I worked with a governor who is being groomed for the presidency in a few years. I wore a wig and pretended to be an additional secretary. That's a laugh because I don't even type."

"Being groomed?" Joe groaned. Was that what was happening to him? "Sounds like a horse preparing for the big race. And you're the woman behind the success."

"Not really," she objected modestly. "I told you, it's up to the individual. In fact, I take cues from my clients. We set goals together according to what they want to achieve."

He grinned and waggled the brochure he still held. "You promise to help them rise above the ordinary."

Marla ducked her head and watched a bubble circle the amber liquid in her mug. "I instill self-confidence."

"Sounds like we could all use a dose of that medicine. Can I keep this brochure?"

"Of course. If you know of anyone who might want any of our services, please pass it on. We can always use the business."

"I will." He glanced out the window, then back. "How long are you staying here?"

"Just until the end of this week. I have to go back Sunday."

Joe nodded, then noticed headlights approaching in the darkness. "That's probably my cousin now." With a reluctance he didn't even try to hide, he made motions to leave.

Marla rose, also feeling a curious reluctance to see him go.

Joe shifted, obviously in no hurry. "I'm probably going to be moving back here for a while and I . . ."

She waited for him to finish, but he hesitated. "To the reservation?" she encouraged, then admonished herself for violating her own pet peeve about rushing the speaker or finishing a statement begun by the other person. It was rude and overanxious.

"Yes." He stroked his chin with his thumb. "I could probably use a course or two that you offer."

"Well, sure." Her heart pounded. He wanted a course from her?

"But I'll call. I have your number on the brochure, don't I?" He extended his hand. "Thank you, Marla. It's been a pleasure. And interesting. Very interesting, indeed."

Her hand rested in his, now warm. "Nice meeting you, too, Joe."

He released her and turned toward the door. The headlights had stopped on the road in front of her cabin. Joe looked back at her just before he left. "I hope we'll meet again."

"Me too."

He accepted her response with no readable expression on his dark face. Inside his broad chest, though, Joe Quintero's heart pounded with hope. He felt as though he *had* to see this woman again. He was compelled, caught in the golden spell of her natural beauty, her self-confidence.

Yet he was also acutely aware that he was too busy to become involved with another woman right now. He had more noble causes to consider, greater challenges to meet, a destiny beyond himself. And he sure as hell didn't need the complication of a woman.

Marla stood at the door and watched the car lights disappear into the night. She turned back to the fireplace and studied the flames as they leaped around the darkened logs, devouring them with blue-white heat.

It was easy to imagine that the brief encounter with Joe Quintero had been a dream. He'd been here such a short time, and now he was gone. There were other things she wanted to say to him, wanted to ask. Marla felt strangely attracted to this man but couldn't avoid the guilt that crept into those feelings. There had been no other man since Wayne, no other attraction.

But this man was different. Joe Quintero was almost an enigma, a woman's fantasy. Marla thought of Joe's expansive shoulders and strong arms, his warm hands and how they'd felt grasping hers in a firm handshake . . . how they might feel touching her; his voice and square jaw and high cheekbones . . . and how it might feel to have his lips close to hers; his muscular body stretched alongside hers . . . making love.

She snapped back to the immediate. Dear God, what was wrong with her? She was thinking . . . dreaming about a man who was a virtual stranger.

Marla turned away from the fire, and her gaze fell on the mug he'd left on the table. There was the proof. Joe Quintero wasn't a figment of her imagination. He had been here in this room. And his memory stayed with her.

ABOUT EIGHT the next morning Marla was awakened by the sound of a truck. She stumbled to the window in time to see a tow truck hauling away the stalled car. Joe's car.

Near noon a knock on the door aroused Marla's hopes that the visitor might be Joe. Just in case, she'd dressed in a red sweater and put on a little makeup. She flung open the door with an expectant smile.

There stood a skinny Indian boy of about seven with jet-black eyes and hair to match. He held out a small package.

"Uncle Joe said to give this to you. And to say thanks for helping him last night." The boy ran away to a car waiting for him on the road.

"What? Wait a minute," she called.

Marla stepped barefoot onto the front porch, expecting—hoping—to see Joe in the car. But the driver was a woman, probably the boy's mother. She waved, a faint smile on her dark face, and drove away. Marla stood there, holding the palm-size box, staring curiously at it.

A gift from Joe. More proof of his existence. Quickly she tore open the box.

Inside, wrapped in plain white tissue paper, was a miniature Apache burden basket, a collector's item made of leather and decorative silver cones. The miniatures had become popular because the large authentic ones were rare and expensive.

Tucked inside the tiny basket was a note.

Thanks for the use of your phone last night and for giving me the spur to rise above the ordinary. You are an interesting lady, Marla Eden.

Sincerely, Joe.

Marla smiled wistfully and pressed the note to her heart. It was so sudden, this yearning, this attraction that she was sure he felt, also. At odd times during the day she picked up the tiny Apache basket and thought of Joe Quintero. She wondered if she'd see him again. Last night he'd seemed sure that it would happen.

With a longing she hadn't felt in years, Marla hoped it would.

2

SMOKE.

It was distant but close enough to sting her nostrils as Marla drove to the post for supplies a few days later. The forest service called them controlled burns, but she knew how fast the flames could get out of control. It had happened several years earlier when a neighboring cabin had burned to the ground before help could arrive. Today the stark chimney still pointed skyward, a lonely sentinel serving as a reminder of the runaway fire every time she passed the site.

She could see a huge cloud funneling skyward like a charcoal genie swirling lighter and lighter against the vivid blue sky, eventually disappearing as a pale gray wisp. There was an ominous power inherent in the dark smoke that invoked a certain fear in her.

Marla pulled her Honda to a stop in front of Berg's Post, a combination grocery store and trading post located at the edge of the High Meadow Apache Reservation. It was a gathering place for the Indians and easier to get supplies there than to travel into the nearest town of Show Low. Mrs. Berg, now a widow, was an old friend who had operated the post as long as Marla could remember.

She approached the beige stucco building and nodded a greeting to a pair of Indian women who were leaving the store. The women's almond-shaped brown eyes and solemn expressions reminded Marla of the exotic appearance of the man she hadn't been able to forget all week. Joe Quintero.

As Marla entered the country store, she instinctively looked beyond the stack of Pendleton blankets to where Joe had been the last time she was here. Of course he wasn't there, and she hid her disappointment with a smile. "Hi, Mrs. Berg. How are you feeling today?"

"Hello, Marla. Nice to see you again. Maria said you were here asking about me. My arthritis is acting up again. I predict we'll have rain sometime in the next twenty-four hours."

"Maybe that's why the forest service is burning today. Did they check with you to see what the weather would do?"

"No. I'd charge them for the information if they did, though," Mrs. Berg said with a laugh. "These old hands are worth a lot."

"They are if they can predict the weather."

"Just the rain, I'm afraid." Mrs. Berg perched on a stool behind the counter. "How long are you staying with us this time, Marla?"

"Until tomorrow. I need a couple of things to keep me going," Marla said as she placed a head of lettuce and can of coffee on the counter. "Let's see. What else?"

"So when will you be back to our woods?"

"As soon as I get another break. Can't stay away for long. You know that."

Mrs. Berg gestured toward the window. "Where're they burning today?"

"Up near the lake." Marla added a can of chili to her small pile on the counter. "I always worry about it going wild. Remember the time McManns' cabin burned?"

"Oh, yes. But I think the forest rangers have learned to control it better now. The McManns sued and won a sizable amount, more than enough to rebuild their cabin elsewhere. I'm sure the government won't let that happen again."

"I hope so. . . ."

"You sound like the folks here." Mrs. Berg started totaling Marla's items and placing them in a bag. "When it comes to burning, the Indians don't trust the forest service, either. Course, they've seen accidents, too. Is that all you need today, dear?"

Marla nodded and counted out the money. "Unfortunately these accidents could cost us our homes. So we're wary."

"Did you know the fire department in Show Low has a new fire truck? One of the most recent models, too. It's a beauty."

"Still, it would take them so long to get around to my side of the lake that the damage would be done." Marla picked up her bag of groceries, then paused, contemplating. If anyone would know about Joe, Mrs. Berg would. She set the bag back on the counter. "Mrs. Berg, do you know a man named Joe Quintero? He's apparently a High Meadow Apache."

"Joe Quintero? I'll say." The gray-haired lady shook her head wistfully, and her blue eyes sparkled with the memory. "Joe and his brother, Josh, were the stuff of legends a few years ago. They were just little fellows when their parents were killed in an awful wreck near Gallup. The boys were sent to Indian boarding school in Phoenix. I think one of the teachers adopted them. An Anglo family, if I remember correctly."

"Adopted Indian children? How could that happen, Mrs. B.?"

"Well, Marla, you must remember it was over twenty years ago and circumstances were different. The Quintero family was poor, and the relatives couldn't easily take in two extra kids. I'm sure they were glad to find someone willing to give such good care to the brothers. And to keep them together."

"That situation would be different today."

"You're probably right." Mrs. Berg shook her swollen, arthritic index finger. "But those boys were given opportunities they wouldn't ordinarily have had. They were excellent students and good athletes. By the time they were in high school, they were in the papers every weekend for winning some sports trophy or scoring a touchdown. They both got football scholarships to Arizona State University. Don't you remember them?"

Marla shook her head. "I guess I was too busy with my own life then to pay attention to a couple of guys playing football."

"As far as I know, they never did move back to the reservation after college. I'll bet the Indians talked about them around campfires for many a year."

"I'm sure," Marla agreed softly. Stuff of legends?

"Why do you ask?"

"I met him the other night." Marla shrugged as if the acquaintance with Joe were merely casual. Well, it *was* casual. "And wondered about him."

The older woman nodded. "I hear he's back."

"He said he lived in California."

"Interested, Marla?" Mrs. Berg's eyes twinkled, and she leaned forward as if to learn a secret.

Marla shook her head quickly. "Just curious, Mrs. Berg."

"I hear that both brothers are very successful men now. Joe is in California and Josh in Texas or Oklahoma."

"We . . . He didn't say what he did."

"I think he's an engineer. But I wouldn't be surprised if he moved back to stay. At least, from what I've heard."

"Why do you say that?" Marla wondered if Mrs. Berg knew that Joe had been right here in the store speaking to a small gathering the day she'd gone to the doctor's.

"Oh, many of the Indians who move away eventually return. Something keeps pulling them back. Don't know if it's their people, their culture or the beauty of the mountains. But it's something powerfully strong."

Marla picked up her bag of groceries again. "The Indians probably would say it's the spirit of the mountains. Or the call of the wind. I can understand, though, because the mountains pull me back, too."

"Guess that's why we're all here, my dear."

"I guess." Marla walked to the door. "See you tomorrow on my way back to Phoenix, Mrs. Berg. Take care of your arthritis."

"I'll be right here, as always."

Marla drove back to the cabin, thinking about two young Indian brothers growing up in Phoenix who now were achieving success in the business world.

Success had always been stressed in her own family. As a result, she and her brother had tried hard to meet their father's high expectations. Maybe that's why Marla pushed herself so hard now—to prove something, even though he wasn't here to see her success. She had fallen short of family expectations when she married so young. Determined to prove herself, she had finished college, even though she and Wayne had barely scraped by during those early years of their marriage.

But they were young and in love and considered themselves invincible. Wayne's illness had smashed their dreams. She was still dealing with Wayne's death when her father was stricken with a fatal heart attack. Afterward Marla stumbled through life, not enthusiastic about anything except her business. She allowed herself no time for playing. Or for thinking about the two men she'd loved so dearly and lost.

The cabin tucked in the mountains was her only refuge and, ultimately, her source of strength. She supposed the mountains pulled her back, just as they did the Indians.

Traveling through smoke that seemed to grow thicker and blacker with each curve, Marla grew increasingly disturbed. Eventually two pickup trucks created a crude roadblock, halting incoming traffic.

"Nobody goes through here, lady." An Apache man approached her car. "We've got a runaway fire up ahead. Need to keep the road clear for equipment."

Marla's heart began to pound wildly. *Runaway fire!* The words throbbed repeatedly inside her head. "I live on the lake! What about the cabins?"

"Looks like only the three at the far end on the cul-de-sac might be in danger."

"Oh, my God! That's where mine is! Please, I have to go in there!"

He peered in the window and assessed her for a moment.

"I'm Marla Eden," she said, gasping. "Mine is the Richey cabin, the one where the lake road curves around. There are only two more past mine on the cul-de-sac."

"Okay." The man waved her through. "Just stay out of the way."

"Yes, I will! Thanks." She gunned the accelerator and flew along the dirt road, making a mushroom cloud of dust behind her car. She had to park a quarter of a mile from the cabin because of the crowd of vehicles already gathered.

She ran the distance to her precious cabin and arrived breathless and somewhat panicky. Smoke was thick, but the fire was still a good distance away. People loaded with digging tools hiked across her yard. Pickup trucks drove around the cabin and toward the woods. Everyone seemed to be moving at high speed while Marla stood frozen and helpless. "Marla! Marla! Oh, my God . . ."

She recognized the stricken faces of two people hurrying toward her. Mr. and Mrs. Banks, a retired couple, had lived in the cabin next door for over ten years. "Are you all right?" Marla hugged them both. "What's going on?"

Mrs. Banks wrung her hands. "Oh, Marla, it's awful! They say the wind picked up and moved the fire faster than they expected. I'm so worried!"

"Now, now, Betty. They've just put us on alert." Mr. Banks tried to reassure both women. "You can see the fire's not that close yet. They've called fire departments in Show Low and St. Johns. And it looks like the forest service and the reservation are sending reinforcements."

"I hope they can contain it," Marla said. "I keep thinking about the McManns' cabin."

Mrs. Banks continued wringing her hands. "Oh, yes, so do I. What a horrible time that was. I don't want that to happen to ours!"

Mr. Banks put a comforting arm around his wife. "Now, Betty, you said you would remain calm."

"But I—"

A new voice interrupted them. "Hey, Marla! I've been looking everywhere for you!"

She wheeled around at the sound. "Joe! What a surprise to see you here!" Marla felt an instant rush of warmth and gratification at the sight of him.

Joe jogged across the yard to where she stood with the Bankses. "I thought you might have gone hiking in those woods."

"I had driven to the post for some groceries." She felt schoolgirlish thinking how she had inquired about him.

"There's supposed to be a roadblock at the highway."

"At first the man there wasn't about to budge. Not until I explained where I lived. I'm glad you're here, Joe."

"It's good to see you, too, Marla. Although these circumstances aren't the best."

Marla remembered her neighbors and introduced them. "Joe Quintero, Mr. and Mrs. Banks. They have the cabin next door."

Joe shook hands with the older couple.

"Do you know more about this situation than we do, sir?" Mr. Banks asked.

"I've just been up to the front line," Joe answered somewhat breathlessly. "The fire's not too close yet. Still a good mile or more away through those woods. But they're anticipating what might happen if it gets closer. That's why you were alerted. They want everyone out of the cabins."

"Oh, this sounds serious!" Mrs. Banks wailed.

"Well, it's serious, but not desperate yet. There's a line of volunteers digging a trench and fire departments from all neighboring towns have been called. Also, I think someone said helicopters were on the way from Phoenix. We'll wet down the cabins just in case."

"Ohhh, I'm so afraid!" Mrs. Banks was near tears.

"Now, now, Betty..." Mr. Banks murmured.

"Tell you what," Joe said with an air of authority. "What I want you to do is to wait at my cousin's house until this is over. There's nothing you can do here, anyway. It's under control."

"I think that's an excellent idea," Mr. Banks responded firmly and nodded at Joe.

"You, too, Marla. Go with them." Joe took her arm. "Please."

"No. I'm staying here." She pulled away and gave him a determined look that said, Don't argue with me now. "But it's nice of you to offer." She turned to her neighbors. "And I think it's probably a good idea for you to go until this is over. I'm sure it won't be long."

Within minutes Joe was ushering the couple toward a dark blue pickup. Marla recognized the driver as the woman who had brought the little boy and the gift from Joe a few days before.

He returned and propped his hands on his hips. "You know you have no business here, either, Marla." He looked bold and powerful in a blue striped rugby shirt with his jacket open down the front. "It's too risky."

"Joe, I couldn't possibly leave. Don't you understand? I have to do something! Should I start unloading the cabin?"

"I don't think that would be a good idea now, Marla."

"What then? I couldn't—" She clutched his arm with frantic fingers. "Joe, I couldn't stand it if something happened to that cabin! It just can't burn down! Please don't let it go up in smoke!" Marla halted and bit her lip. She was afraid of losing control. Then he certainly would insist that she leave.

Joe's voice was calming. "It's going to be all right, Marla. We're doing everything we can."

"That isn't enough! I want—I *have* to do something!" She took a deep, shaky breath. "Oh, Lord, what if . . ." She lifted pleading eyes to him.

"It won't. We won't let it." He gestured toward a group of people. "Tell you what. Let's see if there is something safe you can do."

She went willingly, eager to be doing something, anything.

He set her to work spraying down the cabin. "Now, Marla, listen to me. I'm going back to join the workers digging along the tree line, but if that fire jumps the trench, you have to leave. We all do. Please don't do anything dangerous like running into the cabin to rescue your stuff. Just let it go and leave. Do you understand?"

She nodded, knowing in her heart that there was no way she could do what he was asking.

His brown eyes were serious. "We'll all have to get the hell outta here. I . . . we don't want any heroics that'll risk your being injured."

She nodded again, jaw clenched.

"Okay." For a moment longer he held her with his gaze. Then he turned quickly and left her to battle alone. The next two hours were a blur of activity. The air was peppered with shouts, the revving of motors as trucks came and went, and the constant wail of sirens from fire engines and police cars and a couple of ambulances there on standby.

When Joe found her again, Marla was supplying drinking water to a group of fire fighters. She handed him a cupful and noticed he'd removed his jacket and tied it around his waist.

He gulped the contents of the cup and reached for another, then halted. "Listen! The choppers are coming! You can hear 'em!"

She looked up, a choking sensation tightening her throat.

They waited in anticipation until the loud, wonderful whir of helicopters reverberated overhead. Happy shouts from the weary fire fighters filled the air as twin helicopters swooped in like giant bumblebees and dropped a thousand pounds of water on the wildly roaring forest fire. The blasts echoed off the surrounding mountains, and more cheers went up.

Someone yelled, "That's it! It's out!"

Tears coursed down Marla's cheeks as she turned to give Joe a spontaneous bear hug. She suspected the fire wasn't over, but at least it seemed to be under control again. They watched the helicopters dump another load of water, then go back to the lake for more. She felt weak-kneed and dizzy and wildly relieved. And extremely grateful.

"Tell me it's really out," she implored in a low, tremulous voice.

"The worst is over, but they'll watch it closely for several hours. We've done just about all we can. They're in charge now."

She issued a tired sigh. Together they walked around the cabin, assessing the damage a dozen trucks and several dozen volunteer fire fighters had done to the yard. Marla sank down on a step leading to the front porch. She pushed a wind-whipped strand of blond hair behind one ear with shaky, dirty hands that left a smudge on her cheek.

"Want me to get your car?"

She lifted her weary head and met Joe's sympathetic brown eyes and nodded. "Would you, please? It's the blue Honda down the road a little way. Keys are still in the ignition."

He nodded, then halted in midstep. "You all right, Marla?"

She licked her dry lips. "I just might cry, that's all."

"Everything's okay. Cabin's safe. The fire's pretty well out." He looked down, suddenly drawn to the smudge on her cheek. He wanted to wipe it off but held himself back. "You can cry if you want to."

"Thanks. Is that permission?" She laughed, a high-pitched, hysterical sound. Suddenly the false laughter turned to tears, and she hid her face with those dirty hands. "Oh, God . . . it almost . . . burned."

Joe sat down beside her and wrapped his arms around her heaving shoulders. Gently he pulled her to him, to the strength of his body, and murmured soft, soothing words.

Marla released her emotions and buried her face against his sweat-stained shirt and sobbed. Fears of losing all those years of love and memories wrapped up in the cabin spilled over Joe.

He held her against him while sobs racked her slender frame. To him she felt thin and extremely vulnerable, and Joe's protective instincts surfaced. But other stronger instincts drove him to want to caress her blond hair with his soot-blackened hands. As they clung together, he realized that only in a weak moment like this would Marla lower her guard with a relative stranger. If he'd met her in normal circumstances, it might take months for her to let him see her true self with her emotions so exposed. Secretly he thought that perhaps this crisis was a small blessing in disguise.

Sniffling, she lifted her tear-streaked face and wiped her nose on the tail of her jacket. Childlike, she drew her cuffs over her eyes and smeared soot on her nose and cheeks in the process.

Joe gazed at her, thinking she was absolutely beautiful, red eyes, dirty cheeks and all. This time he succumbed and wiped a smudge from her face with his thumb. Her skin felt like silk.

"I was so scared," she murmured.

"It's practically over now."

"Everybody was great. They all pitched in and worked so hard, even though it wasn't their place."

"They're neighbors. And it's their forest, too."

"I appreciate their efforts. And yours. Thanks for coming, Joe."

"If you're okay now, I'll get your car." He shifted and reluctantly moved away from her.

"When you get back, come on inside. I'll fix you a cup of coffee."

"You sure you want to bother?"

"Of course. I'm fine now. I promise not to break down again." She stood and forced a faint smile. "Coffee is the least I can do to show my appreciation."

"You don't have to do a thing. I need to go soon." He checked his watch. "But sure. A quick cup." He jogged away.

Marla was brewing coffee when he knocked lightly and stepped inside the front door. Her tears were gone, as were the soot streaks, but her face showed signs of crying.

Even so, he thought she was beautiful. Joe was aware that he'd seen her in a rare and unusual situation. This wasn't the same woman who taught people how to act in public, how to keep their cool, how to speak clearly and distinctly. This one had cried helplessly on his shoulder and, for a brief time, needed him.

"Your yard's a mess."

"I know. It'll take some work, but at least it isn't charred like the woods." Marla indicated the scene beyond the window where blackened, stark trees were visible in the distant forest.

He looked around. "Ugh, it even smells like smoke in here. And everything's covered with soot."

"It's everywhere. I have my work cut out for me in here, don't I? But I don't care about the mess. I'm just glad it was all saved. To me that's all that matters." She looked emotionally drained. "It's been quite a day, hasn't it, Joe?"

"Want me to leave so you can rest?"

"No, please don't." Her response was spontaneous, perhaps a little too quick. But she meant it.

He moved into the kitchen. "Your groceries."

"Thanks." Quickly she wiped the kitchen counter. "Put them here." As he lifted the bag, she noticed that his shirt was torn. "Oh, dear, your sleeve's ripped."

He stretched one arm to inspect the tear, exposing nutbrown skin. "Doesn't matter. It's an old one."

"I'll . . . Let me pay for a replacement."

"Wouldn't hear of it. Anyway, it went for a good cause."

"I don't know what I would have done if this place had burned. I'm so glad you came to help."

"When I heard yours was one of those in danger, I was especially concerned."

She gave him a little grateful smile and filled mugs with steaming black coffee. "Cream or sugar?" She poured some cream into hers and waited for his response with hand poised.

"Neither. Thanks." He took his cup and followed her into the living room. "You have a lot wrapped up in this house, don't you, Marla?"

She nodded mutely, then murmured softly, "I didn't mean to let down like that and cry on your shoulder."

"Don't apologize. It was an emotional release. Perfectly natural."

"I—" She looked up at the mantel where she'd hung the burden basket he'd sent. "I forgot to thank you for the burden basket. It's beautiful, but you didn't have to do that, Joe."

"It's just a small token of appreciation. I wanted you to remember the Indian guy you met late one night at High Meadow."

"I'll remember." She set her cup down on the coffee table and paced around the living room, occasionally swiping a line of soot from a piece of furniture. She paused by the huge fireplace, imagining it standing alone amid smoking charcoal posts.

Joe's gaze followed hers. "Looks like it could last forever."

"My father built it of native rocks. My brother, Rob, and I helped him gather them. It took us the better part of one whole summer. I lost ten pounds in the effort." She paused and chuckled. "This is silly. You don't want to hear—"

"Yes, I do. You need to talk about it, Marla."

"But you don't need to listen."

Joe walked over to her and touched the back of her hand with his fingertips. "I want to."

She looked up and saw the sincerity in his dark eyes. And she was spurred to recall the happy memories. "That autumn Dad hired a stonemason from Show Low to help him build it. I remember when we lit our first fire that winter. We had a party and roasted hot dogs on sticks." She chuckled. "Then we made those gooey things with marshmallows and chocolate mashed between graham crackers."

"S'mores?"

"Yes, that's it."

Joe loved to see her laugh. "Sounds as though there's a world of memories here."

"Good ones." She walked around the room, touching things.

"You have some fine Indian art, too."

"My father's collections."

"When did he pass away, Marla?"

Marla looked up at Joe, surprised. "How did you know?"

"I asked someone about you."

She accepted his curiosity about her with a little smile. It was nice to know that their interest had been mutual. "What . . . what else did you ask about me?"

"If you were married."

"Oh?"

"I figured you weren't, but you never know. It wouldn't do for me to be interested in a married woman." Certainly not now, he thought. An Anglo woman might present enough problems. But a married one? No way.

"You're interested?"

He nodded. "I was curious about why you wore a gold band on your right hand."

"And?"

"I learned you're a widow."

"Does that satisfy your curiosity?"

"Not by a long shot. Why do you still wear the ring?"

She shrugged. "I just couldn't put it in a drawer. It meant too much at one time."

"Sounds like it still does."

She didn't answer for a moment. "Time has eased that pain."

"But not the memories." He set his cup on the mantel, walked to the window and stared out. "Do you, uh, have a special man in your life right now?"

She sat on the edge of a chair and sipped her coffee. "Look, Joe, I stay pretty busy traveling."

He mulled over her comment and gazed quietly out the window. So was she saying for him not to bother?

"What about you, Joe?"

He looked up, startled that she would ask. "Uh, no. There's no one special."

"Well, now that we've established availability, I should warn you—"

"I know," he interrupted. "You aren't interested, right?"

"It isn't you, Joe. I just don't have much time for a social life."

"Meaning you don't allow much time for it."

"Something like that." She traced a line along the wooden chair arm, then realized she was drawing in soot, not dust. "Oh, good heavens! This place is filthy! Don't sit down. You'll ruin your clothes." She hurried into the kitchen. Returning with a wet sponge, Marla began to wipe furiously at the chair.

He moved closer, bending down to her level. "You know, Marla, it would be easier if you lived in California. Or here."

Her gaze met his steadily. "I, uh, my business is in Phoenix. But I come up here several times a year." She smiled gently. "Look me up if you're ever in town when I am."

"I can tell you this. Meeting you has already complicated my life. When I go back to California, I'll dream about the beautiful blonde I met in the White Mountains." The serious lines in his face had eased, and his ebony eyes twinkled.

She grinned. "And I'll be dreaming about the dashing Apache brave who saved my cabin from disaster."

"I'm afraid you'll have to include half the High Meadow tribe plus the forest service fire fighters, the Show Low Fire Department and a number of volunteers in your dream. I wouldn't be the lone hero here."

"To me you are."

He struggled to keep from taking her in his arms. She could claim she wasn't interested in him all day, but he read the signs differently. And he knew how he felt right now. Fighting a tender desire for her, he rose and moved to the mantel.

Marla finished rubbing off the chair as if they hadn't come within a hair's breadth of kissing.

Then Joe spotted a small photo of Marla arm in arm with a handsome young man. Instantly his ardor cooled. "How long, uh . . ." He gestured toward the picture.

She glanced up, then continued to wipe the chair. "Wayne died five years ago." There was a time when she couldn't talk about her former husband without falling apart.

Joe shuffled his feet. "You probably find this hard to believe after my admitting an attraction to you, but I'm sorry, Marla. You obviously loved the guy very much."

She nodded. "Fate doesn't discriminate, does it? My father had a fatal heart attack the next year."

"And after that you threw yourself into your business."

"I discovered how working long hours can leave you so exhausted that it soothes heartaches and obliterates memories."

"Or masks them."

She shrugged and sat where she'd been wiping. "Maybe. But it enabled me to go on. For a while I thought I couldn't."

"You're a strong woman, Marla Eden." He took a seat in the chair opposite hers.

"Don't sit there. I haven't cleaned it yet."

"It doesn't matter. I'm a mess, anyway."

She touched her coffee cup, fumbled with it, then pushed it aside. "I asked someone about you, too, Joe."

"Oh?" He leaned forward and propped his elbows on his widespread knees. His hands almost touched her knees, and he wanted to reach out to her. But he didn't. "And what did you find out about me besides my folks' accident?"

"That you and your brother were sent to Indian school in Phoenix. In high school you excelled in sports, then went to ASU on an athletic scholarship and became a successful businessman in California."

"Did you also learn that I never came back to my heritage? To my people?"

"No. Is that important to you, Joe?"

His dark eyes narrowed. "Sometimes I think about it. Think what they need. What I have to offer. And it's important, yeah."

"So what are you going to do about it? Are you coming back?"

"Probably."

"Are you saying you want to contribute, to do something for your people?"

"Sounds sappy, doesn't it?"

"No, not really. But what would you do up here? Where would you work?"

He shook his head as if he had no idea. Sighing, he pushed himself to his feet. "I wish I could stay longer, but there's too much to do before I leave. I'd like it if we had a little more time together before we have to part, Marla."

She looked up at him and surprised herself. "Me too."

"I can't tonight. Plans . . ."

"That's okay. Another time, Joe." She figured his last night was committed to a woman. After all, it was only natural. Marla smiled wryly at her momentary jealousy and stood up beside him. He towered over her. Dammit, this was it. Quick to attract, quick to part.

"I have commitments I can't break."

"It's okay. You don't have to explain anything to me, Joe."

"But I want to, Marla." He touched her hand.

She tingled with warm signals that seemed to radiate from that spot of contact. Her breath caught in her throat, and she fought to hide her reactions. It was absolute craziness, this damned palpitating heart business every time she was near him. But she couldn't help herself. Then Marla did something very uncharacteristic for her. She reached up and kissed him briefly on the cheek. "Thanks for everything," she said softly.

Joe responded by leaning down and kissing her, too. But his kiss was planted solidly on her lips. "My pleasure," he murmured after a moment. Then, with a power beyond his control, he pulled her close and his lips claimed hers again.

This time there was no mistaking the embrace was sparked by the passion of a man for a woman. Marla could smell the smoke that had permeated their clothes and skin as she was drawn against him. She knew his masculine power, and the sensation excited her. Sparks of long-hidden passion began to explode deep inside as she responded to their closeness. His lips felt warm and supple as they covered hers, his tongue tantalized the curved lines of her mouth. And she wanted to open for more of him.

Suddenly Joe raised his head, breaking their contact. His voice was low and ragged. "Till next time, Marla."

She could think of no quick comeback and merely smiled faintly and tried to catch her breath. She'd been overwhelmed by this man and her own response to him. Silently she followed him to the porch and waved as he drove away. Marla was suddenly overcome with the most desperate longing to race after him.

Yet an inner voice told her realistically that they'd never see each other again. She knew it was entirely likely since her business kept her in Phoenix and traveling frequently. And his work kept him in California or here in the White Mountains.

Hell, given the odds, it was probable that they'd never have this chance again. After all, they were both busy and moved in different circles. No chance of their paths crossing.

Goodbye, Joe Quintero.

She turned away from the sight of his borrowed pickup disappearing down the road and faced the extreme loneliness of her own life. In the distance was the sound of thunder. It would be raining soon. But it didn't matter now. The fire was out.

3

MARLA'S BUSY LIFE returned to normal with meetings, out-of-town business trips and absolutely no contact from Joe Quintero. She went to Dallas for three days, then on to Houston promoting Speechcraft Inc. Back in sunny Phoenix, she breezed into the office Monday morning, and dropped four new files on her secretary's desk. "Morning, Letty. Give me a few minutes to get organized, then come on in for letters to these new clients. We need to work out a potential schedule for them, too."

Letty smiled up at her ambitious young boss. "Good morning, Marla. How was Texas?"

"Fine. Busy. I'll give you details later."

"Looks like you spent the weekend working again." Letty bent her graying head over the folders Marla left her. "Already have new client profiles made?"

"How else can I get anything done?"

"There's always the regular work week. Five days is enough for the rest of us."

Marla shook her head quickly. "Not for me. Too much to do. And see how far ahead we are? We're ready to start working with these new clients."

"Don't you ever rest, Marla?"

"What are you, my mother?"

"Mother-substitute," Letty said with a gentle chuckle. "I have a feeling your mother is too much like you to fuss about your workaholic life-style."

"She is," Marla confirmed with a satisfied smile. "She learned the values of working hard first and taught me. Is Kay in yet?" She nodded toward the office of Kay Barlow, her assistant.

"No. She called to say she'd be a little late today. Randy has a runny nose and the day care wouldn't let him attend sick. So she's arranging for a neighbor to take care of him."

"When she gets here, let me know. We have to consult on these new clients. Two of them want general Speechcraft seminars, and I think she should do them. Another wants an individual speech consultant. It'll be good experience for her." Marla walked toward her office door, leafing through the mail.

"There were several messages over the weekend," Letty said. "I left notes about them on your desk."

Marla entered her large-windowed, roomy office. The pastel Southwestern decor provided a feeling of space, even though it was full of tall bookshelves that lined two walls with a small seating area tucked into one corner. Her desk, a huge, L-shape creation, allowed her to spread out her numerous projects.

"Letty?" she called. "What's this?"

"I knew it," Letty muttered under her breath. "Are you talking about the election committee? Listen to the second message on the answering machine."

"Uh-huh. What election committee? City, county, state or...bigger?"

Letty brought a cup of steaming coffee laced with cream to Marla's desk. "I don't think it's anything very big. That's all that was left on the recorder." She flipped the machine on and played back the message in question. "They even set their own appointment time. Nice, huh?"

"Uh-huh." Marla sipped her coffee standing up. "The election committee seems quite sure of itself. It's a good thing there isn't anything else scheduled at nine o'clock. Otherwise 'the committee' would just have to wait."

"Right. Sounds as though he has an accent. Maybe Hispanic."

"Or Indian."

Letty raised her eyebrows and shrugged. "You would know more about that than I, Marla." She returned to the outer office, and precisely at nine she buzzed the intercom. "Ms Eden, the election committee is here to see you. And you were right."

"Send them in." Curiously Marla stood up and waited for the mystery guests who had failed to identify themselves on the recorder but who had made their own appointment.

In a quiet flurry three dark-haired, impressive men entered her office. They were dressed modestly, except for the outrageous chunks of turquoise jewelry they wore. Bola ties, belt buckles, rings and watches were outstandingly decorated with the blue-green gem. The three shook hands with her, and Marla offered them seats.

Politely they declined and continued to stand in a semicircle around her desk. Marla stood, also.

"I am Albert Swimmer," the eldest man began. "This is John Cody. And Phillip Alchesay. We are members of the election committee for the High Meadow Apache Tribe."

"It's nice to meet you," Marla responded. So it was *that* election committee. Her mind whirled. But why in the world would these men want to see her? Did it have something to do with her cabin? Or the fire? Instinctively she waited for the men to state their case.

"We are supporting a new leader for our tribe," Albert Swimmer continued. "One who has the interest of his people at heart. One who knows the ways of his people and will not go against them. One who is smart like the coyote and wise like the eagle. One who can teach his people new and better ways to do things, yet who knows the value of keeping the old traditions." He paused and looked at his companions. They nodded in agreement.

"Yes, I understand." Marla nodded solemnly, too.

"The man we have chosen to lead our people is wise in many ways, but he has no experience in making speeches or in speaking to the television and radio. He is an Apache who knows about the white man's ways. He wants to learn how to work with the Anglo community as well as the Indian. Can you teach him these things?"

As they talked, Marla realized this election committee was considering hiring her to work with their chosen candidate. They could see the value in having a leader who could speak to the media with relative ease and the necessity of being able to move between the two cultures. It was always difficult to change from being a private person to a public figure. Even in the Indian community that was a big step. Immediately she was intrigued with the concept.

Marla gave Albert Swimmer a direct, businesslike gaze. "That's the purpose of my business. I do workshops for business groups or individuals. In fact, I've worked with many candidates for public office, including governors and senators who are now in office."

Mr. Swimmer raised one hand. "To be an Indian leader is different. We do not want a white man's version of a leader. But we want our candidate to be a good representative of his people. This is a time of working together, the Anglo and the Indian, and our leader must be able to do that."

"I can assure you, I have nothing to do with personal philosophy or direction. I teach my clients the mechanics of speaking and conducting themselves in difficult situations, not in what to say. In the end, what they do with my instructions is up to them."

The eldest Apache nodded. "Good. That is good. That is what we want. You teach him the correct way to work, and his heart will show him the correct way to act in the best interest of his people."

Marla smiled. If only life really worked out that way, every client she taught would be a dynamic leader and his or her heart would do the rest. Unfortunately every individual was human, subject to his or her limitations. Marla fully believed that her clients functioned better in public spheres after taking her courses. She couldn't work miracles, however. She gave no guarantees of success.

"I'd like to talk to your candidate before we make any final decisions. We'll see if we can work well together. Also, I have an assistant. Sometimes she has a better rapport with a new client. You can let me know later if you want Speechcraft's services."

"We have already made the decision. Our candidate wants to work with you." Albert Swimmer fumbled in his coat pocket and drew out an envelope. He took a step forward and laid it on Marla's desk. "We will pay for this teaching. But we want it kept between us. We do not want anyone knowing, especially the papers."

"I understand. Most of my clients work this way. You have my assurance that any of our meetings will be confidential."

"We are willing to send you to another place to meet with him in private."

"Oh?" Marla raised her eyebrows, thinking the remote Apache reservation was sufficiently private. "Where?"

"To a quiet place in Mexico. A little resort in a fishing village. Our candidate will meet you there in two weeks. There you can teach him in private."

"Mexico?" Marla took the colorful brochure Albert Swimmer handed her. "It looks lovely. But why so far away?"

"To keep it a secret until he is ready."

"But . . . this is a little extreme, isn't it? Why not somewhere on the reservation?"

The Indian spokesman drew himself up and looked her squarely in the eyes. "You don't conduct secret meetings in your own backyard, do you?"

"Well, no—"

"We couldn't do this in secrecy on the reservation. People would know."

"I see." Marla nodded. He had a point. While the reservation seemed remote to most, it was well populated by the Apache.

"We will send you a plane ticket. Our client will meet you there."

"But if I don't meet him beforehand, how—"

"You will know him. You have already met him."

"I have? How do you know?"

"His name is Joe Quintero. He is our choice for the next leader of the High Meadow Apache." The expression in Mr. Swimmer's sharp, dark eyes accentuated his words. "If you do your job, Marla Eden."

"Look, there are no guarantees here."

"You just do your job, Ms Eden. And he will do his."

Marla nodded mutely, and the men filed out of her office. She could hardly believe what she'd heard. A million questions raced through her head. She was sure Joe was behind this visit from the committee. But why? Did he really need

her services? Or was this his way of getting them together?
The man was certainly surprising.

She recalled his parting kiss as a taste of passion. Sweet and
seductive. Whetting her appetite for more. She smiled, remembering that, secretly, the experience had left her shaking with desire.

Letty poked her head in the door. "I'm dying of curiosity.
What did they want?"

Marla motioned to her secretary. "You'll never believe this,
Letty." She leaned back in her desk chair and started laughing. Clutching her heart, she twirled the desk chair around
and around, laughing like a fool.

"Marla . . ." Letty looked at her boss strangely.

"It's all right, Letty. You're going to get your way at long
last! I'm going to Mexico with a very handsome man!"

"What?"

"Get this. The 'election committee' is a group of High
Meadow Apache working to elect a new leader. They're hiring me and sending me to a remote resort in Mexico to work
with their candidate! Now can you beat that?"

"I've never heard of such a thing."

"Do you remember my telling you about Joe Quintero?"

"The handsome Apache who helped fight the fire at the
cabin? Oh, yes."

Marla nodded. "He's running for chairman of the High
Meadow Apache tribe. The man has never made a public
speech. And he's never been on television. He wants me to
teach him!"

Letty beamed as she watched her young boss twirl the chair
around again. It had been a long time since she'd seen Marla
so happy.

JOE QUINTERO SMILED as his attractive assistant, Kendra McGee, entered his office. "Come on in and have a seat."

She referred to a notebook. "Maxwell and I couldn't come to an agreement on the phone, so we set up a meeting for tomorrow to discuss their project. I'd like you to be there. And your brother returned your call while you were out. He said he'd call again later."

"Josh?" Joe shook his head. "Damn! We've been missing each other all day. I'll try again in a little while. But first, you and I need to discuss some changes, Kendra." Joe rose from behind his desk and opened a cabinet door. He brought out a bottle of bourbon, usually reserved for clients, and set it on one end of the desk.

Kendra McGee looked curiously at her boss.

"I've decided," he said simply.

"I figured," she answered tightly. "I'd be lying if I didn't admit to spending my share of time worrying about this, Joe."

He got ice cubes from the small refrigerator in his office and dropped them into two glasses. Then he sat back down and gazed distractedly at the items. "During all this I've learned that it's very important to me. More than I realized when the tribal committee approached me to run for chairman. I want you to understand, Kendra, that to me it's serious business. At least now, at this point in my life, it is. Maybe at another time I wouldn't be willing or able to spend four years on such a project."

Kendra tugged at the hem of her skirt. "I'm not making any judgments, Joe. This is your heritage and your business, and I respect both."

"Thanks. Means a lot to have your support." He looked steadily at her. "I know this probably sounds crazy, Kendra, but I've decided to take their offer and go back. I'm going to run for the office of chairman of the High Meadow Apache."

"I'm not surprised," she said with a little smile. "But, Joe, what will you do about the company? Four years is a long time and you have twenty-five employees dependent on Quintero Engineering."

"That's why I called you in today. I'm not going to throw away all I've—we've—worked for here. But I want you to understand what I'm doing and why. And I want you to run the company until my term of office is finished."

Kendra gave a little gasp of surprise. "You . . . you mean it, Joe?"

He nodded confidently. "I'm positive. I've thought about this long and hard, just as I've thought about my decision to return to Arizona. I've worked with you for five years now, and I've watched you carefully. I like the way you manage, the way you handle crises. I think you'll do a fine job." He stood and splashed a little bourbon over the melting ice, and handed one glass to her. "Furthermore, I expect you to accept the challenge."

She reached out a shaky hand. "I don't know what to say, Joe."

"Say yes."

She nodded. "Of course, yes!"

He smiled and clicked his glass to hers. "Here's to our challenges, Kendra. Yours and mine."

Kendra stood and returned Joe's toast. "I think you're wise, Joe. And I like your decisions."

They laughed and Joe directed her to the small conference table in the corner. "Let's figure out how we'll manage this, Kendra. I won't be completely inaccessible. I'd like to be a part of the major decisions. For instance, I'll arrange to attend monthly meetings. . . ."

The two put their heads together to work out a plan, and when Kendra left, it was almost dark. But they had a satisfactory strategy for handling the business.

Joe looked at the notes scattered on the table, the charts, the new schedules. He knew this whole endeavor was risky. His future was unpredictable. That alone was scary. But also exciting.

Stuffing his hands into his pockets, he walked to the window. His view included proof of affluence and signs of further expansion stretching endlessly over the southern California hills. In either direction were fields of newly constructed office complexes, condos, town homes, high-rise apartments. The growth was inevitable and out of control.

After two weeks in the remote White Mountains of Arizona, Joe felt closed in and trapped in California's civilization. He wanted open spaces and lofty mountains thick with timber. He wanted to see the eagles flying free and feel the wind's power in his face. The phone interrupted his thoughts, and he reached for it.

"Quintero Engineering."

"Hey, Joe! How's it going, bro? I got your message to call, but hell, you're never there!"

"Josh!" Joe smiled at the sound of his brother's voice. "It's about time we connected. How are things in Oklahoma?"

"Looks like my team is heading for a losing season. Doesn't bode well for the coach."

"Too bad. And you thought they had potential last spring. How are things with you and Judith?"

"Funny you should ask. She, uh, left last week. This time I think it's for good."

Joe sighed. His brother's marriage had been on the verge of collapse for months. "What about Mick?"

"I will fight not to lose custody of my son; surely you know that."

"I don't blame you, Josh."

"What's going on out there on the high-tech coast? Have you decided?"

"Yep. I'm going to do it."

"You have my admiration, Joe. Not many men would dump a successful business in California to go live on an Indian reservation. Even if it was for a good cause."

"I'm not dumping anything. Kendra is taking over. I've seen the way she works, and I trust her. She can handle Quintero Engineering as well as anyone."

"Sounds like you have it all worked out."

"Not quite. I need a campaign manager. One I can trust."

"Are you offering me the job?"

"Who else? A coach with a losing season and a marriage on the rocks should get out of town."

"Hell, Joe. I don't know anything about election campaigns."

"But you know me. And you understand our heritage. And I trust you."

"I'm choking up."

Joe laughed. "Well, they're looking for new blood, new ideas."

"New blood, huh?" Josh chuckled. "Well, I guess that's me."

"All right! Look, we need to get together to make some plans. Why don't you fly out next weekend?"

Joe finished the conversation with his brother and hung up with a satisfied sigh. Things were beginning to fall into place. He was convinced that with thorough planning it could work. He needed Josh as his right-hand man, needed someone who understood this quest. He wanted someone who wouldn't question his motives but who would know that returning to the White Mountains was something he had to do.

Inevitably Joe's thoughts turned to Marla Eden. She, too, would help him achieve his goals. But would she understand his motives? He clenched his fist. That didn't matter. She would teach him the skills he needed. He told himself that her personal feelings were unimportant.

He recalled her beauty, pale and delicate. Her blond hair, floating freely in the wind; her smile, tempting; her brown eyes, alluring. The touch of her lips had jolted him to the core, and remembering made him long to feel them again. He could hardly wait for their rendezvous in Mexico. Just this morning he'd received a call confirming her acceptance.

Joe smiled. It had taken some persuasion, but he had convinced the election committee that he needed her. And he did. He'd never felt more sure about a woman in his life.

4

HER PLANE WAS LATE.

Joe paced in front of the spacious windows of the small Mexican airport, occasionally checking the thick, low-hanging layer of clouds. He approached the ticket counter for the third time in twenty minutes, unable to mask his uneasiness. "Excuse me, sir. Can you give me any information on the plane from Phoenix?"

The ticket agent didn't even look up from his newspaper. "She is late, señor."

"I can see that. Do you have any idea when it will arrive?"

"She is storming everywhere. Very bad."

"Has the plane taken off from Phoenix?"

"I do not know, señor."

Joe's frustration mounted with each of the agent's seemingly indifferent remarks. "Well, what the hell do you know?"

The man shrugged and rattled the paper as he turned the page. "She is raining, señor."

"She sure is." Joe muttered and stalked away. He stood by the window, one hand stuffed in his pocket, the other impatiently twirling a yellow rose. Rain pelted the runway, making tiny pockmarks in the sheet of water that covered it. He'd arrived yesterday, before the weather fell apart, to a warm, sunny Mexico. Dammit, why couldn't the weather be nice for Marla's arrival?

He thought of her, a woman who'd captured his imagination from the beginning. What would she be like as he got to know her? Would the spark they'd both felt last month in the mountains still be there?

It was another hour and a half before the local airport staff began moving about, indicating on a crude bulletin board an incoming flight originating in Phoenix. Joe felt some degree of anxiety as he watched the plane emerge from the low ceiling of gray-white clouds and splash down into the sheet of water. It was with great relief that he recognized Marla making her way down the steep metal air stairs. She dashed across the tarmac through the pouring rain, each footstep splashing water knee-high.

Standing in the customs line with the other passengers, she threw back the hood of her beige raincoat. Her blond hair had been neatly tucked into a knot, but several tendrils had worked loose and hung in soft waves around her face. She was beautiful, and he felt more than sparks as he waited for her. It was all Joe could do to stay on the far side of the barrier, away from her.

Marla spotted Joe and gave him a little wave of recognition. She could hardly wait to get out of the tiny terminal and be with him. It was a long-anticipated moment that was delayed even longer for passport checks. Now, after running through the rain, she was wet and cold.

Water squeezed between her toes, oozing around inside her pink pumps as she stood in line. Dammit, why had she worn them, anyway? She would have been better off barefoot. At least she wouldn't have ruined her new shoes. Trying to disregard the unpleasantness, she assumed her well-trained, confident bearing and smiled at Joe, who waited so impatiently across the terminal.

The way he paced the tile floor reminded her of a caged tiger. In the month since they'd met in the White Mountains, she'd forgotten how handsome he was, how large and powerful he looked compared with those around him. Yes, Joe Quintero would make an imposing candidate for the Apache.

She'd also forgotten how much his strong masculinity appealed to her. Or perhaps she'd been successful in pushing those thoughts to the back of her mind. Until now.

Today he was devastatingly informal in pleated white trousers and a heavily textured white cotton sweater. He wore leather haurales—Mexican sandals—on bare feet, and his copper skin contrasted with his entire outfit. He'd let his dark hair grow a little so that it edged his collar. His expression was serious, almost brooding, and his eyes were like onyx, shiny but intense. In one large hand he toyed with a single yellow rose. There was only one word for him today—*sexy*—and Marla couldn't avoid thinking it, try as she might.

When Marla finally walked through the customs gate toward him, Joe felt a strong impulse to wrap his arms around her and greet her with a kiss. A long, meaningful kiss. But he was too reserved and felt that now wasn't the time or the place, so he handed her the rose with a smile. "Welcome to sunny Mexico, Marla. I'm afraid the sun's taking a siesta today."

Marla took the flower, touched by the romantic gesture. "Why, thank you, Joe. What a nice, but wet, welcome."

"All day I kept telling myself they must have rain to produce such beautiful flowers this time of year." His sweeping gaze took in her hair and the rain-spotted shoulders of her raincoat. "But why did it have to pour today?"

They moved out of the stream of traffic and stood facing each other. She tucked a damp strand of hair back into place, but it returned to droop beside her ear in a loose curl. "I'm soaked. I must be a mess."

He breathed in her faintly floral fragrance and found her wildly alluring, especially in her slightly disheveled state.

Decent conversation became a struggle. "You're lovely...er, you're just fine. Did you have a rough flight?"

"Wasn't the smoothest. Did you have to wait long?"

"Couple of hours."

"I'm sorry, Joe. Wish there had been some way to warn you about the delay."

"No trouble. Seeing you is worth the wait." He quickly amended his statement. "Seeing you down safely. Although I'm sure everything was under control. It's just that when you're waiting and don't know what's happening, it's nerve-racking."

"You should have been tossed around up there," she said with a little chuckle. "Not fun."

"Believe me, I thought about you . . . about your flight and wondered if it was rough." His expression was serious, then he broke the strain with a little smile. "Well, now that you're here, we can both breathe easier. Do you have luggage?"

"Lots, I'm afraid." She smiled apologetically. "I try to travel light, but I had to pack more clothes than usual because I'm staying so long. And, of course, the video equipment."

"Video equipment? Just for me?"

"It's part of the Speechcraft training, whether there's one or fifty-one," she explained. "After we've been through some of the strategies and I've taught you a thing or two, I'll make a video of you and we'll see how much you've learned. We have to have a VCR to play it on, so I brought one of those, too. Figured they wouldn't have one in the room, and getting one might be difficult."

"You're right about that. Even TV reception is poor." With his hand lightly on her back Joe guided her to the edge of the crowd awaiting luggage. "The whole thing sounds complicated."

"Not really. I simply use the wonders of electronics as one of several learning tools. It helps both of us decide quickly what improvements you may need to make. And we work on them together. It's a process that I'll explain more fully later."

"I'm impressed already."

"Joe, I want you to know that I'm honored to be chosen to work with the Apache candidate." She smiled genuinely. "This is one of the most important assignments I've had, and I've either put things on hold or turned them over to my assistant in order to give you my best effort."

"I rank that high, huh?" His dark eyes twinkled with a touch of light.

"You bet. And I appreciate your recommendation to the election committee."

"You understand, I hope, that I really want . . . no, I *need* your help, Marla." He grew serious again. "I don't have any experience in the areas of communications, especially the public kind. In my business there was no need for it. The incumbent's opposing me in this election. And Ben Cartaro's been doing this for years. Kissing babies and making speeches comes naturally to him."

"Those are learned techniques," she said with a wily grin. "And I'm sure you'll be speaking with ease in no time. You have a lot of natural ability." She had dreamed about his natural ability, but it had nothing to do with speech-making. Now, though, she had to forget that and get down to business. Joe's future could well depend on her. It was a sobering thought.

"Speaking naturally? Sounds like a minor miracle to me."

"You're going to do great." She thought that if he appeared as he was today, so earnest and bold, and so damned handsome, he'd win on intent alone. "The pressure's on me. I'm the teacher, and I'll only feel I've done my job if you're elected, Joe."

He laughed. "You sound like a very determined lady. What's the old saying about turning a sow's ear into a silk purse? But I'm sure glad you're on my team."

As they waited for her luggage, Joe experienced her closeness in a strange way. He felt as though invisible ties were wrapping around them, drawing them together. This was the work of fate, to thrust them in the same path and put them to work on a joint project. This is where they belonged. He wondered if she felt the same, if she believed in fate.

Or was he attracted to her because of her striking beauty and because she said all the right things? She certainly made him feel as though what he was doing was the most important thing in the world. That took a special skill—and a very smart lady.

When her luggage was finally stacked on the sidewalk, Joe dashed through the rain and returned in the car he'd rented.

Marla laughed when she saw the bright yellow Volkswagen bug. "You're going to get all this in *that* little thing?"

"Just takes some packing skills," he said as he tucked a bag under each arm. "I worked in the stockroom of a toy store one summer. I can arrange anything to fit." He hefted another bag and began stuffing them all into the tiny vehicle. When every spare inch was filled, he opened the passenger door and, with a flourish, made a mock bow. "Madam . . ."

"I'm impressed with your packing skills," she said with a teasing smile and squeezed into her seat, arranging her long legs as best she could.

"Sorry, but this car is all I could find to rent yesterday," he apologized as he slid in beside her. "They don't have a wide choice of rentals here. They like VWs. No leg room but cheap to run."

"This is fine. Gives us a challenge. You've already met the first one by getting all my luggage in here." She was well aware of how snugly they fitted into the small vehicle. Shoulders rubbing, elbows occasionally banging and knees separated only by the stick shift on the floor.

"Actually, the first one was getting me in here," he said with a chuckle. Joe made a special effort to keep his eyes—and hands—on the gearshift as they took off through the rain. But he was acutely aware that the front panels of Marla's coat had fallen open and of the way her skirt had crept upward on her shapely legs. And he could hardly take his eyes off those long legs that were tucked so modestly beside his.

Once, reaching for the gear, he brushed her leg with the back of his hand. He wasn't sure whether to apologize and bring attention to the incident or ignore it. He couldn't ignore the slide of his hand over her smooth hose, and he shifted clumsily so that the car lunged.

In an effort to divert their attention, he related information about the area. "The airport is located between Guaymas and the beach town of San Carlos. Our villa is on the beach, but Guaymas is a larger city, well-known for fabulous shrimp. If you like, we'll drive over there one day for some."

"Love it."

"You probably know that fish and seafood dishes are the main staples around here. No tacos or hot chili or what Americans think of as Mexican food."

"Well, that makes sense, this being a seaport."

"You'll have to try the turtle, too. It's great." He peeked through the narrow slot above her piled luggage. "Too bad you can't see the beautiful scenery as we drive to the beach. There are mountains on the right side of the road, the bay on the left. Flowers everywhere. It's beautiful."

"Sounds like a lovely place to work," she said as they rounded a curve and their shoulders pressed together. His muscles felt hard and unyielding, and her fantasies of the man she'd met in the mountains returned full force. "What a good idea to come here to work." But suddenly she wondered if it was such a good idea. All she could think of at the moment was the man beside her.

Joe grew silent as he concentrated on driving the rain-slick road to their Mexican villa. He realized his frustration with the rain and the delayed plane and even the modest little car were signs of how much he wanted this whole experience to be perfect for Marla. They could work in private almost anywhere. But to be alone in Mexico with her was the ideal, the reality of a fantasy, and he wanted it to be special for both of them. But she didn't seem to mind the inconveniences nearly as much as he.

When they arrived at the villa, Joe insisted that she go on in while he unloaded her baggage in the rain. Reluctantly Marla complied. She found a glass for the rose in the kitchenette and placed it in the center of a round pigskin table by a window. Vaguely she wondered about the view. Joe had said they were right on the beach, but all she could see were gray storm clouds.

Wandering through the casita, Marla found it to be first-class with all the modern conveniences, tiled floors and bath, a sliding glass door in the bedroom that opened onto a garden patio, a kitchenette and a living room. She hung up her raincoat, freshened up a bit and returned to the living room.

Joe was ordering room service by phone. "Hot coffee for two, *por favor*. With lots of cream." He looked questioningly at her. "Anything else? I'm starved. Didn't have lunch. You hungry?"

She shrugged and remembered she hadn't eaten, either. "Anything," she whispered.

"And a basket of sweet rolls," he added, then caught her eye again. "Would you rather have a drink. Wine or—"

"No. Coffee's fine, thanks." Marla stepped around the pile of luggage Joe had left in the corner.

"And some cheese soup and tortillas," he continued, then hung the phone up slowly, his eyes glued to her, his mouth slightly open. She was stunning in a pale pink knit dress with matching shoes. And oh, those legs! This was a different Marla from her blue-jeaned casualness in the mountains. Different, but just as fabulous.

Eyeing the pile of baggage that filled the corner, she groaned aloud. "I see I have my work cut out for me."

"Not now. You're in Mexico. That job can wait until *mañana*." He waved her toward the cozy seating area that consisted of a small sofa and two chairs flanking a low wooden table.

"I'll need to unpack them before we can go to work."

"There's plenty of time for that. Come on and relax now. The coffee and pastry will be here soon. We can unpack tomorrow. I'll be glad to help you." He didn't want her to feel pressured into working right away. It was the only way he could think of to make up for the day's inconveniences.

"Joe, are we the only ones here?"

"For now, yes."

She walked slowly toward where he sat. "You mean you don't have anyone in your, uh, camp? No one came with you to work on political moves or the campaign or...anything?"

"My brother, Josh, is coming down in a week or so. Does it bother you that we're alone?"

Her eyes met his. "No..." Even though she denied it, there was doubt in her tone.

"I came down here to get away before the push of the election. And to concentrate on our work together. I thought you understood that, Marla."

She sat down opposite him, her hands in her lap. They were alone in Mexico. It hadn't occurred to her that they'd be completely alone here or how she'd feel about it. This training session was very private, indeed. In fact, it was beginning to look more and more like a rendezvous. "But we *are* going to work—"

"Absolutely! But not this minute. I figured you'd need a little time to rest after arrival. Tomorrow will be soon enough. And even then I hope it won't be a big push. We're in Mexico, remember. Everything's laid-back here."

Marla smiled, vaguely thinking that concentrating on work with him would take some doing on her part. "Of course."

"In case you're wondering, I'm staying in the next casita," he said, motioning with his thumb. "But there'll be no problem with privacy, if that's a worry. Our doors don't join. We'll have to hike over the sand to get together, uh, to meet for work." He nodded toward her bedroom. "Did you look around? Does the place meet your standards?"

"Oh, yes. It's very nice."

"I figured a casita with a kitchen would come in handy. That way, we, er, you can fix some meals. But my campaign will pick up the tab, whether you eat here or out."

"That's fine."

He leaned back. "Relax, Marla. You've had a tense day, but you're here now and everything's okay. Mexico's a good place for unwinding. It's a state of mind, so they say."

Marla sighed. "It *has* been a long day." He was right. She was tense and it always showed. Some of her Speechcraft strategy was to teach clients how to release their tension. She wasn't very good at practicing what she preached. At least not today.

Looking at Joe, she wondered if he even needed a lesson. He was so damned magnificent sitting there on that sofa with his arm stretched across the back of the empty seat next to him. He looked very relaxed, she admitted privately. How she'd like to curl up beside him in the shelter of his arm.

"And I'm sure you had a stressful flight. At least waiting for it was stressful on this end."

Her expression softened as she realized perhaps he wasn't quite as cool as he appeared. She leaned back and crossed her legs, then noticed her wet shoes and sat upright again. How could she have forgotten them? She'd have to blame her preoccupation with her newest client. "Oh, damn! Look at my new shoes! They're soaked! I'll bet they're ruined."

"Take them off so they can dry. Maybe we can get someone around here to work on them." He leaned over and easily tugged one high heel off, then wrapped both large hands around her damp, cold foot. "Your foot's like ice."

Her mouth went dry. "Your hands are warm." A cocoon of heat from his hands embraced her foot immediately, and a tingle of electricity raced up her spine. "Ohhh, nice . . ." Her breath caught in her throat as energy radiated from him to her miserable foot and up her leg. His action left her rattled, and her own sudden reaction to his erotic touch was startling. She hadn't been shaken like this since becoming a widow and it was unnerving. Yet she couldn't move away.

"You'll get sick sitting around with such cold feet," he admonished in a gently commanding tone. "Take your other shoe off. Come on, give me your foot."

Obligingly she switched legs so that he could remove her other shoe, which he did after tucking the shoeless foot next to his thigh.

"Doesn't that feel better?" He had stripped off the offending shoe and was massaging the toes and arch of her chilled foot. "Move it around. Get some circulation going."

Marla took a shaky breath and wiggled her toes. Her foot began to tingle. "Yes . . . yes, it feels much better."

While one large hand cupped her heel, the other rubbed every inch of her slick, stockinged foot. It was heavenly. As the feeling returned, she became aware of the strength and heat of his muscled thigh, where the other foot was snuggled. For a wild moment she had an intense longing to inch that foot along his muscular leg.

She leaned back again and tried to breathe normally while his hands manipulated first one foot, then the other. It was seductive and she was all too receptive.

"How's that?"

"Wonderful." She struggled to maintain a sensible conversation as the tingling sensations crept up both legs. "I waded through ankle-deep water on the airport runway."

"Too bad they didn't have jet bridges straight from the plane to the terminal to keep you dry." His fingers circled her ankle and pushed up toward her calf.

She swallowed hard. "Actually, sometimes I think we're spoiled in the city with everything so convenient. That's one reason I like to go to the mountains occasionally. It's good to get back to the basics. Makes you appreciate everything more."

His dark eyes smoldered with passion as he continued to hold her feet in a cozy bundle. "Sometimes it can be refreshing. Other times, terribly harsh. Like now. I wanted the casualness of Mexico. And the sunny beaches. But I hadn't planned on rain."

His palm pressed the length of her foot, and the pressure spiraled to her rapidly pulsing heart. "What had you planned on, Joe?"

"I wanted it special for you."

"It is—"

The moment was shattered by a knock on the door.

Marla was torn between wanting his ministrations to end quickly and a wild yearning to scoot closer to him. No, it *had* to end. They were there to work.

"Must be room service," Joe muttered, reluctantly releasing her feet. "Do you have some warm slippers?"

She chuckled to hide her nervousness. The huge yellow fluffy things made her feet look like Big Bird's. "They're not very glamorous."

"Are they warm?"

She nodded, thinking nothing could possibly be as toasty as his hands on her feet. "They're fuzzy inside."

"Get them, then. I don't care about glamorous. How does coffee sound right now?"

"Like heaven." Marla scurried across the cold tile to find her slippers while Joe answered the door. She'd lied. His hands were like heaven; coffee was a poor substitute.

He set the tray on the table between them and poured them each a cup of coffee. Soon they were hungrily munching the various types of sweet rolls and sipping cheese soup.

"It's great, Joe. Every bite is delicious. I didn't realize how hungry I was."

"This is more like it." He helped himself to another golden-baked, fruit-filled *empañada*. "This is what I had in mind for you. For us."

"Joe." Marla's brown eyes met his with a sudden intensity.

"Yes?" He took a bite of the fruit pastry.

"You set this up, didn't you?"

He finished chewing. "Hmm?"

"You know what I'm talking about. This . . . this rendezvous in Mexico. It was your idea for us to be alone, wasn't it?"

"How else could I get you to make me over and turn me into an orator?"

"We didn't have to come to Mexico for that. I thought I was here to do a job."

"You are. So am I. Look, Marla. There was no other way. Don't you see that?"

"No other way?"

"Of getting to know you and still accomplishing my goals."

She pushed a strand of hair behind her ear. "Somehow I feel I'm one of those goals."

He sat forward and leaned his elbows on his knees. "Not so. I hired you to help me accomplish something bigger than either of us. If you don't feel that way about my challenge, maybe we'd better get it straight now."

She watched the intensity grow in his ebony eyes. "Frankly, Joe, I think you can do whatever you want to, with or without me."

"Maybe. But I'd rather not. I happen to think you can help me where I'm weak."

"Weak? You, Joe?"

"We all have our weaknesses. One of mine is in the area you know so well. Public communications. The other happens to be you, Marla Eden. I think . . . you're beautiful." He pushed himself away from their cozy setting and walked to the window, which was dark by now. "I'm only human."

"So am I," she responded quietly. "Joe, you realize this could be dangerous, mixing business and our personal lives."

"It could be." He turned his head and gazed steadily at her, his eyes demanding an answer. "Can you deny that you feel anything when you're with me?"

Her eyes met his, and she knew she had to be honest with him. There was no other way with Joe. "No."

His sigh of relief was barely audible. "Good start."

She shook her head. "Risky business."

"Even if there are no obligations beyond our business together? And no demands, I promise. Volunteers only."

She looked at him doubtfully, then a smile slowly spread across her face. "Volunteers?"

His expression was quite serious. "Two volunteers. One won't do it. Not for me, Marla."

"Me either, Joe."

He smiled and seemed relieved. He walked back to where she sat and poured more coffee. His large hand covered the cup as he drank from it. "Let's get one thing straight, Marla. I need you. I'm not ashamed to admit it. I need what you can teach me. I'm looking forward to it. I hope you are, too."

"I am." Her voice was low and somewhat strained after their exchange. "That's why I came here in the first place. I was intrigued with the nature of the job as well as the client."

He smiled and rose again. "I'm going to leave and let you get settled and warm. I recommend a hot bath." He picked up her wretched pink shoes, suspending them from two fingers. "I'll see what I can do about these."

"Thanks." She stood and approached him slowly. "Just volunteers, right?"

He nodded. As she drew closer, he could feel her presence closing around him. And he had to fight to keep from pulling her into his arms. "Right."

She reached out and touched his arm. Then she went up on her tiptoes and kissed his cheek. "Tomorrow we work."

"Mañana." He bent forward and caressed her lips lightly with his, fighting all the while to keep from hauling her against him and devouring her with his desire. As he moved away, his eyes met hers, barely concealing the passion he held in tight control. *"Buenas noches,* Marla."

"Good night, Joe."

JOE HUNCHED OVER the bar in the restaurant that was attached to the villa. He drank Bohemia beer from the bottle and toyed with the idea of asking Marla to dinner. But he decided against it. Too much, too soon. He had to think. And she needed time. He ordered her a bottle of wine, instead.

He tried to keep his emotions from ruling his head. What he wanted from Marla was all of her, selfishly to himself, her complete attention and affection. What he wanted was the impossible.

She had her career and her life, both of which were so different from his. He wanted his new career challenge and her, too. Impossible.

If he'd had any reservations about her, he'd received his answer today. The bolt had hit the minute he saw her in the airport. And after spending just a little time with her and even kissing her briefly, he knew the flames kindled inside him were definitely greater than a spark.

And yet, even as he thought of Marla, his mind shifted to his campaign and the difficulties associated with his possible election. There were also tribal problems and what to do about the economic struggle of his people. Give in to the developers' ready answers? Or... what?

Joe paid for his beer and walked out into the misty night. If he became involved in a relationship with Marla now, she would have to share him. As much as he'd like, he couldn't be completely, totally hers. He was already committed to another goal.

And was that fair to her?

WHEN SHE EMERGED from her refreshing bath, Marla was delighted to discover that Joe had sent her a bottle of California Chardonnay. Curled up on the sofa where he'd sat, she sipped a small glass of wine and let her thoughts wander.

She noticed the yellow rose he'd presented to her in the airport and realized the gesture had been somewhat romantic. Perhaps he even had seduction in mind. He had been honest enough to admit his interest in her. And she had reciprocated.

Being with him this evening had been so easy, so natural. And she hadn't been able to resist kissing his cheek before he left. But when his lips had touched hers, the feelings that had spun through her couldn't be denied. She hadn't felt this way with anyone since Wayne's death, mostly, she suspected, because she'd been successful in avoiding any intimacy with a man. Until now.

But Joe was different.

Though she was reluctant to admit it, Joe made her feel desire again . . . the rich, strong desire of a woman for a man. She wanted to hold him close, to feel his heartbeat and to feel him inside her. And she wondered if she could spend another day—or evening—with Joe and keep their relationship strictly businesslike.

5

"I KNOW. I'm too early."

"What makes you think so?" Marla blinked sleepily and drew the front panels of her yellow robe tighter across her breasts. "I'm usually at work by now. The leisure of Mexico must be getting to me already." She couldn't avoid staring at Joe, not fully prepared for her reaction to the sight of him this morning.

Dressed in a red sweatshirt and black running shorts, Joe exuded a mild musk as he panted on her doorstep. His hair fell in dark disarray around a red headband. His tanned, muscular arms were magnificently displayed by his cutoff shirtsleeves, and his powerful legs glimmered with a thin moisture sheen. The aura of a healthy heat radiated from his body, bringing a warm flush to hers.

He swiped a drop of sweat from the tip of his nose with the back of his hand and reached up to brace himself on the side of the doorframe. The man emitted unbridled masculinity that almost took her breath away.

Joe's smile was more of an openmouthed admiration. Finally he spoke. "You look like—"

"Don't say it. A canary, right?" Marla's laughter was still husky with sleep. "My sister-in-law gave me this outfit last Christmas. It's my favorite color, but this is a bit much, don't you think? Trouble is, it's comfortable and warm." She stuffed her hands deep into the pockets and wriggled her shoulders beneath the thick material. "And I just love the way it feels."

Joe watched her movements and rubbed his jaw with his thumb. "I don't think you look like a bird. You look terrific to me." He thought the bright yellow enhanced her blond hair, but a canary wasn't his comparison. His thoughts ran more to a glass of bubbling, intoxicating champagne. "I was going to say that you look like you just crawled out of bed. I woke you, didn't I? Sorry about that."

"It's okay. I should be up by now. This is the first time in ages I've slept this late." She squinted in the bright sunlight. "You probably want to get started early."

"I already did, running along the beach."

"You've been out already? I'm really late."

"No, you aren't. It's just a little past eight. This stretch of the beach is a great place to run. You don't have to get up at dawn to avoid the crowds. It's practically empty most of the time."

"How appropriate that you're a jogger." Her lashes fluttered as she took in all of him. "I read that ancient Apache runners used to run four miles with a mouthful of water to test their endurance."

Joe's mood changed immediately. His relaxed attitude and smiles were gone, and the brooding expression returned to his dark eyes. "Reading up on how to handle this Apache?"

Marla's heart sank, and instinctively she put her fingers to her lips. Stupid! She'd offended him with her unthinking remark. It was presumptuous of her to relate Joe's jogging to his Apache ancestry, of which he was obviously sensitive. On the other hand, his reaction pointed out his hypersensitivity, something the media could manipulate or give unwarranted attention to in the name of news.

She stuck to her guns. "No, Joe, I wasn't reading up on you. I think I read that fact in Arizona history when I was a kid, and it stuck with me. I was impressed with that kind of endurance."

"I'm not an Apache runner. I'm just a man who jogs to keep in shape."

"Joe, I'm sorry if I offended you. I didn't intend to. Please believe that. I didn't think before I spoke. Will you accept my apology?"

He nodded, but his face remained tight and expressionless.

She gazed up at him, trying to read his impassive facade, finding it impossible. Spontaneously Marla reached out and squeezed his hand. He responded with a little flinch, but he didn't move away from her touch.

Marla let her hand remain on his for a moment. "Aside from the Apache long-distance runners, I'm also impressed with anyone who jogs. I'm more of a walker. It's less jarring to my body than running." She paused and he had no comment, so she cleared her throat and continued. "I suppose you stopped by this morning to see when we should get started working."

"Actually, I stopped by to remind you that I'll help unpack all those bags. And to see if you wanted to have breakfast together. As soon as I grab a quick shower."

"Well, I'm not much of a breakfast fan, but..." Marla moved her hand from his and pushed her disheveled hair back. Of course, he probably wanted a business breakfast. Inadvertently her gaze traveled beyond his broad shoulders to the sunlit stretch of sand and water. Soft waves rippled against the shore, and the salt air smelled fresh and clean. Suddenly everything else was forgotten, and she moved outside into the glorious sunlight. "The beach! It's right here!"

"I told you the Marisol is located between the mountains and the beach." He gestured behind them where the white stuccoed villa with its red curved roof tiles was nestled against a rugged mountain range that followed the shoreline.

She whirled in a circle to take in the scenery, smiling and hugging her arms. "It's wonderful, Joe! Really beautiful!"

His mood softened as he watched Marla's response to the place he'd chosen specifically for her. "Didn't the election committee give you a brochure?"

She looked chagrined. "Honestly, I glanced at it but didn't pay much attention. I travel so much, I figured it was just another hotel."

"Just another job, huh?"

"I have a feeling that when I leave here, none of this will be just another anything, Joe."

"I'll do my part to help you remember."

"Oh, I'll remember."

He shifted and rested his hips on the low porch railing in a half-sitting position. Behind him stretched an endless extension of blue from the softly swelling Sea of Cortez, or Gulf of California. This was a sight she'd long remember.

"Did you sleep well? Any disturbing noises or problems with your rooms?"

Marla pretended not to notice his muscled body so boldly revealed in his jogging outfit. She was *trying* to think business while he was looking like a copper-skinned Adonis. And she couldn't keep her mind off the man.

"I slept like a baby," she said with a grin. "The casita is great. It reminds me of my cabin in the mountains, so peaceful and quiet."

"You like it, then?"

"Love it! I can hardly wait to walk on the beach!"

"Before or after breakfast?"

"It would be nice to go now while it's still early. Well, sort of early." She inhaled deeply. "Doesn't the air smell delicious after a storm?"

"Yeah, I was just noticing that." He glanced at her quickly and saw the beginnings of a smile.

"Forgive my faux pas, Joe? Even speech consultants make mistakes."

"Sure. Forget it. Get your duds on, and we'll go walking."

She smiled happily up at him. "You want to go along? After jogging?"

"It'll be a good cool-down for me."

"Okay. I'll only be a few minutes."

"Mind if I come in and get a drink? I don't run with water in my mouth."

"Not at all." She ducked her head at his reference to her remark about the Apache runners. Maybe this was his way of dismissing her mistake.

By the time she emerged dressed in white shorts and a blue pullover, he'd called room service for orange juice. They gulped the fresh-squeezed juice and were off to romp along the seashore. Sometimes running, sometimes walking, they laughingly soaked up the sun's energy. For over an hour they frolicked in the sand, enjoying the simple pleasures of searching for unusual shells and dodging the incoming ripples.

"This is the real reason people come to the seashore," Marla declared as she stooped to pick up a faded orange whelk.

"To walk along the beaches? To smell the ocean? To get lost in time? To find their own perspective in the scheme of things?"

"You're certainly philosophical this morning. I'm talking about something much simpler. To find the perfect channeled whelk." She turned the shell over in her palm to reveal the corroded underside. "Obviously not this one." She tossed it back into the sea. "But the search goes on for the perfect shell, one that time and the sea hasn't battered."

"Why the whelk?"

"Because it's so difficult to find a perfect one. The whelk isn't like a clam, all flat and plain. It has spikes on the outside and intricate spirals on the inside that make it unique. I'm sure they're harder for the sea creature to make than a simple clamshell. That's why, when you find a perfect one, it's very special."

Like you, Joe thought as he let her lead the conversation as well as their walk. Perfect and special in many ways. And unexpected, as he was discovering.

By the time they turned around and headed back, Joe had grabbed her hand and was racing with her in and out of the water. Breathless, laughing, shoes wet and bare legs splattered with sand, they reached the casitas.

"Surely you're hungry now." His statement sounded more like a question.

"I'm starved! Nothing like a walk on the beach to whet an appetite."

"Great. Meet me in thirty, then."

She nodded. "That'll barely give me time to shower and call my office."

"Okay, make it forty-five. I probably should do the same. Be careful, though," he warned.

"Why?"

"Don't sound like you're having too much fun."

"I wouldn't want that." She grinned over her shoulder. "This is, after all, a business trip."

Joe watched her disappear and trudged slowly across the sand to his casita. Marla filled his mind, tantalized his thoughts and dominated his fantasies. She had many sides, both business and pleasure. Maybe there was a way to integrate a relationship so that it included both and wasn't unfair to either of them. That's what he'd work on, anyway.

During her shower Marla's sense of obligation returned full force. She met Joe dressed in khaki slacks and a tailored blouse with beige and white stripes.

He wore navy walking shorts, a powder-blue shirt with white piping and hauraches. She swallowed a comment on the tip of her tongue about how great he looked and kept reminding herself this was a business breakfast.

"What's this?" He indicated the flat leather briefcase tucked under her arm.

"I thought we could get started during breakfast."

"Good idea." They walked along silently, and he wondered how much actual work they could accomplish over eggs and coffee. But she was in charge here, and he was impressed with her. And usually surprised.

In the restaurant he followed her past hanging baskets filled with tiny purple-tinged orchids to a patio table overlooking the Sea of Cortez. Between the fresh fruit cup and main entrée, she opened the folder devoted to Joe and got out her pen.

"Okay. This is just preliminary, Joe. Sometimes it helps me to learn a little about you before we start goal setting." She looked down at her notebook. "In some respects, I feel as though we've known each other for ages. Yet I don't even know what your business is, Joe."

"Engineering. About as removed from politics as can be."

"Have you ever held a public office? Councilman or committee chairman?"

"Not even PTA president."

She made a note. "Hmm, not much experience."

"Not in the public arena. You have your work cut out for you, lady."

"That's okay. I expected a challenge." She moved her papers to make room for a plate of *juevos chorisos*, eggs scrambled with a spicy sausage. "That's what I'm here for."

"Now seems to be a good time to tell you that I've never made a public speech to more than ten people. And they were people who worked for me, so they didn't dare laugh. Or question me." He paused to take a bite of eggs. "I've never stood on a podium and looked out over a sea of strange faces, except to receive a football trophy and mumble something stupid."

"Does the idea that now you'll have to make many public speeches like that scare you?" She glanced up, pen poised.

"Speechless."

She rolled her eyes at his pun and paused to start on her eggs. "Maybe it'll help you to know that most people are petrified at the thought of speaking to a crowd. It's the number-one fear in the business world. But then, some people are hams and get a charge out of being the center of attention. It's important for me to know which is your category so we can go from there."

"The former, definitely."

She made note. "Hmm."

"Can you help me, doctor?"

"I'll try."

"Can you do something about my sweaty palms? And those butterflies in the pit of my stomach that make me feel as though I'm going to toss my cookies? And the rubber legs that make me walk like I've had too much hooch?"

She laughed. "Believe it or not, most people, especially those who have a great deal of anxiety, joke about the matter."

"Oh." He groaned and dropped his forehead to his hand. "You've seen through my act."

"You're just typical, Joe."

"That's no better. I want to rise above the ordinary. Your brochure promised."

"That's something you'll have to do when I'm finished." She gave him a secure smile. "But I've no doubts about your ability."

"I'm curious about how you expect to cure this anxiety disease." He buttered a corn tortilla and rolled it into a finger shape before taking a bite of it.

"I may not be able to cure you completely, but that isn't necessary. Sometimes nervous energy can be channeled and put to good use when addressing a crowd. My aim is to give you sufficient techniques and skills to boost your self-confidence so that you're assured you can handle whatever might occur."

He smiled devilishly across the table at her. "Come on, now, what's your secret? Do you go along to hold your client's hand for the first speech? Or put cucumber compresses on their brows and chant a few magic phrases?"

"Obviously you've thought of some cures that I haven't. My job is to prepare you to go out on your own by teaching you a few tricks that may work."

"Tricks, huh?"

She made a note, then proceeded, taking an occasional bite of her breakfast. Learning about Joe was far more interesting at the moment than food. "What about the news media? Have you ever been interviewed by a reporter or been on the radio or TV?"

"Nope." He snapped his fingers. "Take that back. In my youth I was on TV weekly. But all I had to do was stand there looking like a young brute in my college football uniform and tell how I tucked the ball and zigged this way or zagged that way until I crossed the goal line. It was fun because I was still high—" he stopped and grinned at her "—high on adrenaline after the game, of course."

"That's what I'm talking about. You'll learn to put that extra flow of adrenaline to work for you." She couldn't help thinking he must have been a handsome young brute in his college football uniform. "Never done anything more, ah, serious?"

"I've never had to answer to anyone outside the company about my business decisions. Never explained my logic to a camera—not that I'll have to in the future, but..." He shrugged.

"But you might. Given today's media interest in native Americans, you probably will at some point. Count on it." She gave him a steady look. "And you will have to realize that you can't be too sensitive about your heritage. Most of the media won't be native Americans, nor will they be as, uh, responsive to your reactions as I. You never know what they'll ask."

He raised one eyebrow. "You think I'm too sensitive?"

"That's a matter of judgment, and not mine to make. It's yours. You'll have to decide if you're going to be the chip-on-the-shoulder Indian leader or—"

"Or?"

She took a deep breath. This was shaky ground, and she hoped she wouldn't foul it up again. "Or one of a new type who is broad-minded and progressive as well as loyal to his people."

"I always took pride that I was that kind of man." He shoved his plate away and propped his elbows on the table. His expression had grown serious. "I guess when confronted with my heritage, I become a little defensive. Maybe a lot defensive. But I won't sidestep my stand. I am Apache." He tapped his own chest. "We call ourselves *Indee*, which means 'the people.' And everything I do will be in the best interest of 'the people,' the Apache, my people."

"That's the way it should be, Joe. I have no intention of changing your philosophy or your stance. But you need to have clearly in mind exactly *how* you want to represent your people. The reason is so that you don't let the media distort any of your stand. You need to remain in charge at all times."

"Somehow this sounds like a battle between them and me."

"No, it's more of a competition for who comes out on top, or who gets the best story. Your job is to give them a story, the story you want them to have. Now, I know how the media will dig, the kinds of probing and insensitive questions they'll ask. My teaching strategy is to play devil's advocate so you can practice with me how you'll respond." She leaned forward earnestly. "But please believe, Joe, I'm not against you. I'm on your side."

"Fair enough." He motioned for coffee refills and sipped thoughtfully as he watched her finish her meal. Maybe Marla was on his side and would be more understanding of his dedication than anyone else could be. And what about fairness?

She certainly sounded as though she knew exactly where he was coming from and what to do about it. She understood him, and that was extremely important to Joe. It occurred to him that perhaps it wouldn't be fair for either of them to resist the attraction they both felt. That could be something very good for both of them, too.

TWO HOURS LATER they sat in the middle of her living-room floor, a cluster of empty luggage around them and various machines and equipment and books and notebooks piled on the tables.

Marla smiled at Joe. "Thanks for the help. It was quite a job to drag all this stuff along."

"Did you pack it all yourself?"

"That part was easy. I had help from my office staff, and we did it over several days." This morning she'd seen another side of Joe, different from the serious, brooding man running for chairman of the Apache. This Joe was warm, had a sense of humor, and an occasional smile that was devastating. And he was honest enough to admit his insecurities. She liked that in a man.

She opened them each a soft drink, then curled up on the sofa, Joe's open folder in her lap. "Ready to start on goals?"

He sat cross-legged on the floor and leaned his back against the chair opposite her. "As good a time as any."

"I've filled out a fact profile on you that will include my evaluation. We'll go over that later."

"Your evaluation? Mm-hmm—can't wait for that."

"My *professional* evaluation. The goals we set today will be what you want to achieve in this course. I like my clients to tell me what they want to accomplish, or what they think they want. We'll discuss the options and how I can help, what I can and can't do. We'll also compare yours with mine. Then as the program proceeds, we can reevaluate and set different goals at any time."

"Okay, my goals." He glanced up and motioned at her notebook. "How much paper have you got there? I have a list of goals as long as my leg."

"Just give me a few of the main ones, as they might refer to this course."

"This sounds hokey, but I want to be the best I can be," he said tightly.

"Joe, I don't consider anything you say hokey."

He studied her for a moment, nodded gratefully and continued. "I'm not trying to achieve perfection, but I think I have a lot to offer. I want the best of that. I also want to make my people proud of me. Now this has nothing to do with pride or arrogance, which is not the Indian way. I'm talking about being a man my people will admire, sort of like the way we try to please our fathers and make them proud. Do you understand what I'm trying to say, Marla?"

"I think so.' You want to be their champion."

"Yeah, that's a good word. Champion." He propped one leg up at an angle and hooked an arm around his knee. "I want to do so many things for my people it's probably unrealistic to think I can do it all. But I'd like to try."

"What are some of the most important things?"

He looked up at Marla for a moment. Rubbing his jaw with one hand, he studied the blond woman who concentrated on her note making. She looked and sounded sincere, and he knew that at some point, considering his overwhelming feelings toward her, he'd have to trust her. The time might as well be now.

"For the new Apache leader, there'll be some exchange, some possible business deals between the Indian community and Anglo businessmen. I want to make sure these deals are handled properly, in the best interests of my people. In the past, our way of dealing with situations that we didn't understand or trust was simply to reject them. But times are different. I want to learn to weigh certain situations and determine what's best. And to know what should be rejected. Are you following me?"

"I . . . I think so." Marla realized she was being tested and that whatever he was talking about was very sensitive and private. "I can give you some general negotiating techniques, if that's what you need."

He snapped his fingers. "Yes, that's it. Negotiating. In my business the deals are laid out and straightforward. You either want it or you don't. None of my decisions will affect the quality of people's lives. That's a heavy load."

"Yes, it is." She made a mental note that he seemed somewhat relieved by her answers. Strangely, she felt as though she was the one being grilled, not him. But a degree of trust had to be established between her and any client. Because of their working so closely together and the power of sensual electricity between them, however, she figured their trust had to be complete. "Any other goals, Joe?"

He looked at her pointedly. "To learn to speak well. I have a lot to say, and I don't want it lost. I want it to reach everyone, as if it were carried on the wind."

"Quite a challenge. But you have good goals. Difficult, but not impossible." She leaned back and studied the handsome man sitting on the floor. "Now let me tell you some elements that I think will work in your favor. This is my professional viewpoint, you understand. Your opinion about your position of leadership is that it's extremely important. That opinion shows in your attitude, Joe."

"Sometimes I think I take it too seriously."

"No. That's good. If I see it, others will, also. That's something that can't be taught. You either have it, or you don't. Your sincerity will shine through your efforts, Joe. For a politician that's crucial."

He nodded. "When I was approached, I felt it was a challenge and an opportunity that I couldn't refuse. They need so much in a leader. I just hope I'm the man to give it to them."

She reached down and pressed his hand in a gesture of affirmation. "Yes, you are, Joe. You're exactly what they need."

He turned his hand over so that their palms matched. Her hand seemed small in his as his long tanned fingers laced with her pale elegant ones. For a mind-spinning moment he was caught in her spell. The sincerity in her eyes, the forward thrust of her breast against her blouse, the sexy way her hair fell over one shoulder, tantalized him. *Am I what you need, Marla?* He reached up with the other hand and trapped a tawny curl between two fingers. "Marla, I think you are exactly what I need."

He rose to his knees and their faces were suddenly level. She didn't draw back, even though his intention was obvious. His eyes darkened and the lids lowered sensuously.

"Joe—"

"Let me kiss you, Marla...."

Although she knew better, Marla couldn't move. She wanted that kiss! She drew in a shallow breath through slightly parted lips.

As if in slow motion his mouth moved closer to hers, hovered for a second as he savored their closeness, then claimed the moist prize waiting for him.

In that magical moment Marla dropped her pen and let the folder slide from her lap and from her thoughts. All her consciousness was directed to the sight and touch of Joe and how spontaneously her body responded to him.

From the mere touch of their hands, palms pressing, expressing deeper desires, Marla felt her reserve melt away. Then with the kiss, one simple little kiss, she felt a swirl of joy, spiraling her feelings out of control. She wanted more than a kiss, wanted to touch him, wanted him to touch her. She pressed forward, inching her hands along his shoulders. His muscles tensed beneath her fingers, and she clutched his shoulders as if she might fall from his embrace.

But Joe had no intention of letting that happen. He wasn't about to let her go so soon. His arms swept around her waist; his chest pressed to her knees. He had her right where he wanted her, where he'd dreamed of having her since their first kiss in the mountains.

His lips played with hers, lessening the initial force of the kiss, sipping gently at the top lip, then the bottom one. His breath was hot and sweet on her lips, and she opened her mouth for the intrusion of his tongue. Marla felt a flush of heat as he continued his sensuous exploration.

Slowly his tongue outlined the shape of her lips, then slipped inside with a gentle thrusting motion. Just when she thought she would die of these prolonged pleasures, his lips captured hers with renewed force. She wanted to open her knees to allow him to move closer, but she became preoccupied with the subtleties of his kiss.

Her body grew slack, and he wedged himself easily between her knees. She could feel the sides of his broad chest on her inner thighs, and automatically she squeezed her legs against him. A delightful erotic swirl rose from the center of her being and pulsed hotly through her. Heart pounding and passion aroused, Marla could only think that she wanted to pull him closer.

There was no more denying to herself—or to him at this point—how she felt whenever they were close. And now, as his lips molded sensuously to hers, as his body sought hers, Marla felt as though everything they'd said and done had been aimed at this glorious moment when they connected. And she never wanted it to end.

Joe lifted his head first: "Oh, Marla, the things you do to me. . . . I seem to be out of control."

"Both of us lost a little control, Joe."

"Lost? Or gained?"

"I told you I think it's risky."

He moved back to gaze at her. His dark eyes seemed like ebony on fire. "It wasn't so bad, was it?"

She smiled faintly. "It . . . it was very good, Joe. But I'm afraid there's no future for us. We both have other commitments that—"

He pressed a finger to her lips. "No, don't say it. The future will take care of itself. Let it happen, Marla."

"I don't know...."

"Then don't close the door before you know for sure." He leaned over to pick up her pen and folder with his name typed on the raised tab. "You might be missing something damned good. I know I will."

She took the folders from him, making a big deal of rearranging her papers. "We have a long way to go down here, Joe. We'd better slow down."

"I was just thinking we didn't have much time." He touched her cheek with such longing that his feelings were obvious to both of them. "Resisting you is more difficult than I thought it would be, Marla. Maybe I'd better go for now."

"For a first day I think we've accomplished a lot." Marla felt flushed and breathless as she followed him across the room. "And thanks for helping me unpack."

"I'm looking forward to lesson two."

"What time do you want to get together tomorrow? I'll set my alarm so you won't have to wake me this time."

"How about tonight?"

"Tonight?"

"For dinner. I understand the Marisol Cantina fixes great shrimp scampi."

"Well, I, uh..."

"Unless you have other plans."

"No, of course not. What plans would I have?"

"Around seven, then?"

She nodded, unable to say no and not really wanting to. But she wondered how she'd make it through more hours with him.

Joe reached for the door, then turned back to her. His dark eyes captured her in their imploring depths. "I want to explain why I responded so sharply about the Apache runners this morning. As a young athlete I was one of those Apache runners in ceremonies on the reservation. I guess your comment hit too close to home and I have no sense of humor about that. But mostly I hoped that you would forget about my heritage when we were together."

"I don't know why I said that. You must know it doesn't matter to me, Joe."

"I want you to think of me as a man first. Just a man."

"I'm afraid . . . that I do, Joe."

"Good." He lifted her chin with two fingers and caressed the tiny indentation in her chin with his thumb. "Don't be afraid of what's happening to us. It can't be bad. It's too good with you, Marla." He lowered his head for another quick kiss. "I've got to go. While I can." He turned. "See you tonight."

"Yes. Tonight . . ." She watched him leave, his arms swinging, his powerful legs propelling him across the sand.

Finally she turned away and squeezed her eyes shut. Oh, Lord, in those few minutes when they'd touched and kissed, she'd wanted that man as she had wanted no other in years. She wanted Joe to take her in his arms, to lay her down right here on the floor and make love to her until she cried out. She thought she'd scream watching him leave her. She wanted to call him back. Wanted him.

Well, she'd see him in a few hours. Dinner and then what? She pressed her fist to her forehead as if trying to force the raging thoughts and feelings from her head, from her being. But it was impossible. Her heart was in control.

6

AFTER DINNER they strolled along the brick sidewalks that laced through the resort. The impact of their earlier kiss lingered, and as if to guard against it happening again, they held hands with fingertips loosely entwined.

Yet even such a light contact sent Marla's senses soaring, and she fought a private preoccupation with Joe Quintero's fingers. They ended up back at the casitas that lined the beach. The moon was visible as a thin, translucent disk, its silver glow reflected in the black night sea.

"Want to walk some more?"

The thought of continuing to move in step with him was somehow provocative and unnerving. But then, to her everything about Joe was provocative—downright sexy. She smiled with an unavoidable eagerness. "But not in these high heels."

"We can fix that easily enough." Joe sat on her porch step and began peeling off his shoes and socks. "Oh, this reminds me. I left your pink shoes at the front desk. Manuel said his sister-in-law could fix them as good as new."

"And I thought they'd never be the same."

He reached for her hand and urged her to the step beside him. "After Mexico nothing is the same."

She gazed into his ebony eyes and saw the dancing light of desire. "Nothing?"

"Nothing or no one is the same after being under this moon. But don't expect to get your shoes back soon. Mexican leisure, remember?"

"I'll be here three weeks. Is that long enough?"

"Sometimes one day is long enough for the change. Or one night."

"I'm talking about the shoes. Long enough to repair them."

"Oh." He grinned. "Probably. I'm sure you won't need them around here. You won't need anything...." He knelt barefoot in the sand before her and grasped one sandal heel. "Like now. These things must go. A person should never walk a beach in shoes. You've got to feel that gritty sand against your arches and between your toes." His fingers stroked the erogenous areas as he mentioned them. Then he went to her other foot, creating the same havoc with her libido. "What's this? The businesswoman has discarded her hose?"

"We're in Mexico, land of sun and sand." She felt breathless and wondered how the simple act of removing shoes could send her into such a spin. "The brochure said 'no hose necessary.'"

"Good girl!" He laughed. "You did read the brochure, after all. Now if I could just get you to discard these high-heeled civilized trappings altogether, we'd be all set."

"I can't be too casual with a client. I'll ruin my professional image."

He took her hands and pulled her to her feet. His lips were alarmingly close to hers as he whispered, "You know what I say to that? To hell with image."

She smiled. "Why, Mr. Quintero, is that any way for a candidate to talk?"

"I wasn't talking. I was whispering something privately to a lady. Now would you like to walk, or go inside and talk further about private matters?"

They looked into each other's eyes, and the air seemed charged with electricity. Joe wanted to take her in his arms. But the expression in her eyes—was it apprehension or fear?—held him back.

"I think we'd better walk." She moved him toward the beach.

Discarding their shoes seemed to be a symbolic act, and they both began to shed any earlier reserve. Joe held her hand solidly, warm palm to warm palm, as they walked barefoot in the sand, letting the grains slide between their toes and push against their arches.

Their pace was leisurely, allowing Marla to search for shells in the moon's pale glow. Occasionally she stopped to pick one up but always sailed it into the water when she discovered a flaw.

"Still searching for perfect whelk?"

She tossed her hair in the gentle night breeze. "Always."

"What if it doesn't exist?"

"I'll just keep searching."

"I can't imagine searching for something that might not be found."

"But I never lose hope."

"No matter how long it takes?"

"I know it's there, out there somewhere, for me."

He halted and she altered her step beside him. They were still holding hands, standing close. He looked into her brown eyes, so like his yet so different. "Marla, what are you really looking for?"

"I told you. The perfect . . ."

He turned his body toward her, and his hands eased up her bare arms. She shivered beneath his feathery touch. "Is anything perfect? Maybe this . . ." Two fingers lightly touched one breast, stroking its rising slope all the way to the tightening tip.

Marla held her breath and tried to keep from responding to his magic. She hoped he couldn't feel her nipple's sharp contraction inside her thin, lacy bra. Suddenly, wildly, she wanted to fling the constricting garment aside and open herself to Joe. But she couldn't. Not yet. She shuddered. "No..."

"Marla, you are a perfectly beautiful woman. Perfect in so many ways."

"You don't know me very well if you think that."

"I want to know you...all of you." He took a step forward, allowing the entire length of his body to mold to hers. He lowered his head, letting their lips merge into a very gentle kiss. His hands came up to rest high on her rib cage while both thumbs massaged tiny circles around her tautly crested breasts.

She couldn't hold her breath forever, and as she released pent-up air, her breasts expanded against his chest. The turmoil within her body grew as desire swirled stronger and faster. She knew she had to stop and rather frantically pushed on his chest. "Don't, Joe," she murmured and stumbled away from his clutch.

He steadied her immediately with an arm around her shoulders. They walked in silence as Joe wondered why she continued to hold back when he knew how she'd responded to him. And he'd made sure she knew of his bold response. The tension was interrupted when he stumbled on a knobby shell and began hopping around, emitting several expletives. "Nails! Or glass! This place is dangerous in the dark!"

Laughing at his antics, Marla felt relief as she picked up the offending obstacle and tossed it into the water. "It's only an oyster shell crusted with barnacles."

"Vicious little critters, aren't they? Now I know why I've never been much of a shell collector. They attack!"

"You run by them so fast that you don't have time to search for and find the pretty ones. That's another advantage of walking. It's slow. You have time to look around."

"And time to think," Joe added.

"Yes, sometimes too much." Marla knew that was why she stayed so busy most of the time. It didn't leave her any time or energy for thinking.

"And what do you think about when you're alone, Marla? If I weren't here this minute, what would you be thinking about?"

She kicked a spray of sand in front of them. "Oh, probably some aspect of my business or my family. Sometimes I ponder about life in general. Where I fit in the scheme of things."

"And where's that?"

"I used to think I was stranded, all alone on an island." Her voice grew pensive. "But I've discovered that my feet are on pretty solid ground."

"I suppose we all feel stranded at times," he said, interpreting her solemn mood.

"Do you, Joe?"

"Yes, especially now. I'm out on that island alone. Not stranded so much as standing alone. What I've undertaken is a tremendous responsibility. But it's my decision, my personal challenge."

"You aren't completely alone, Joe. I'm in it with you. My goals are yours. I told you I won't be content until you're elected chairman of the Apache Nation. And I'll always be available for any future help."

"As my own private consultant? Thanks. Y'know, it's funny." His voice was low and thoughtful. "Here you are a non-Indian and my main ally."

"I can't believe that. I found my friends and family invaluable when I needed them."

"Most of my friends are Anglos in California, and they don't really understand. That's why you're so unusual. And my family is supportive, but from a distance."

"I thought you said your brother was going to help with the campaign."

"Yes, Josh will be a part of this endeavor and head up my campaign. I'm not sure that even he understands, though."

"And your other family?"

"They're divided into two camps. My adoptive parents are Anglo and live in Phoenix. They're proud of me, but my father has been in poor health, so his participation is quite limited. My Indian relatives are cousins, uncles and aunts. They're enthusiastic about my return to the reservation but are a little distant because they don't really know me well."

"Your work is extremely important, Joe. Sometimes work takes the place of people."

"That's a strange thing to say. Is that what you've done, Marla? Put your work in place of people?"

"I desperately needed the work, the preoccupation."

"So you became a workaholic."

"I accomplished my goals. My business is successful and growing. And my sanity is—" she laughed "—still somewhat intact."

"What about your family? What do they say about your obsession with work?"

She laughed. "I come by it naturally. They're workaholics, too, especially my mom. She doesn't even take time anymore to go up to the cabin."

"I'm glad you do. I would never have met you otherwise."

"I can't stay away. Something keeps drawing me back. The mountains give me a kind of strength. Sounds mystical, doesn't it?"

"My uncle Will would probably agree with you. Does your family live in Phoenix, too?"

"Yes, although we're scattered in different areas. I live in Scottsdale. My mother is in Carefree. She has a new career in real estate and a new gentleman in her life. We're still adjusting to that, although he's very nice, and she seems happy with him. My brother, Rob, is married and lives in Tempe. He and Phyllis are expecting their first child in the spring. We get together occasionally, but they have their own lives and . . . I have mine."

"Which is . . ."

"Mostly work. But," she added quickly, "it takes that kind of dedication to make a new business successful. You know that, Joe."

"And there's no one else in your life?" He couldn't help wondering if she had another lover and that's why she seemed so intent on resisting him. "No love interest?"

In the uneasy quiet that followed they could hear the gentle lap of the waves caressing the shore.

"No. I haven't wanted—"

He slowed his step. "Until now?"

She slowed with him and waited before answering. "Until now."

He stopped completely and turned her to face him. "Marla, look at me. I haven't been involved with a woman in a long, long time. But when I first saw you in the mountains, I knew. Since then I've been able to think of no one else. Of nothing else but having you. . . ." His hands rested lightly on her shoulders. "For a while I tried to stay away. This is really bad timing for me to get involved with a woman. But I can't help it. Do you understand? Do you believe me?"

"Yes, I . . . I've thought of you, too, Joe. It's the first time since . . ." Her voice quavered, and as he drew her closer, she placed her palms on his chest. Somehow the pounding of his heart reassured her, for she knew it was pounding for her. He wrapped both arms around her and held her in his embrace for a long time. He was strong and secure, and she knew she needed a man like him.

When they started walking again, they were headed back toward the casitas. His arm rested across her shoulders, and her arm circled his waist in the back. It was comfortable, an easy way to stroll, arms hooking their bodies together, hips rubbing, side by side.

"What does your brother think about your returning to the reservation, Joe?"

"Josh thinks I'm nuts." Joe chuckled. "But he's taking a year off his job to manage my campaign. Actually, he's taking a year out of his life since he's in the midst of a nasty divorce that involves child custody for his son, Mick. You'll probably meet him next week when he comes down for a strategy session. We'll be coordinating schedules and discussing plans. He wants to issue some press releases. Maybe you could help with that since it has to do with communicating and the media."

"Be glad to." She was quiet for a moment, then decided she had to know. "I can't believe there's no woman in your life, Joe."

"I'm divorced. It happened a long time ago. No kids. It just ended and we parted." He paused, then decided to add, "I'll admit I've spent the weekend with a few women since. But none I cared about. I, too, have been building a business."

They walked the rest of the way to the casitas in silence, arm in arm. When they reached Marla's little porch, they stood in the sand, bare toe to bare toe, fingers laced, clinging to the moment.

"Thanks for dinner, Joe. It was wonderful. And the walk in the moonlight was . . . marvelous." She couldn't begin to tell him what his kisses had done to her. "Actually wonderful is an inadequate word. And marvelous is overused. I can't think of the right—"

"How about extraordinary?" He leaned forward and kissed her. "Magnificent." Another kiss. "Remarkable."

"Yes, all that," she murmured between kisses.

"And more. Excellent, jim-dandy, super-duper—"

She laughed aloud and he kissed her again, molding his lips to hers, barely dipping his tongue inside, then pulling it back. Once they touched and were caught in each other's embrace, there was no parting, and they drew closer, completely wrapped together, lost to everything save the sounds of each other's heartbeats and the gentle lapping of the waves against the shore.

The night breeze picked up and sent her shivering against him. She put her cheek to his and whispered, "Don't leave me yet, Joe."

"Wouldn't think of it."

"Let's go in. I have that bottle of wine you sent last night."

"Wine . . ." He caressed the silkiness of her cheek with his fingertips as if trying to absorb her softness. "Couldn't be as intoxicating as you." Turning her face up to his, he kissed her again, this time with great tenderness.

She led the way inside and poured them each a glass of the expensive Chardonnay.

They raised their glasses, clinking them together without words. Clichéd quotes seemed out of place now. They sipped silently, dark eyes exchanging expressions of smoldering passion.

Joe examined her face for an answer to his unasked question as he tried to control the desire that raged through his body. Working with Marla today and being alone with her tonight had brought them closer. He knew more about her. Knew—more than ever—that he wanted her. And now thinking that they would soon sleep in separate beds drove him crazy.

"Marla, I—"

"Would you like to have a seat, Joe?"

"No! I want—" He halted and lowered his voice. "Marla, you know what—"

"Would you like to stay awhile?"

He glared at her from across the room. He was serious. Why the hell was she smiling? "Yes. You might say that. I want you."

She turned away from his intense gaze, reading what was on his mind. It was on hers, too. "Yes, I know."

"And you, Marla? What do you want? I think we're of the same mind. Or am I misreading the signs?"

"No, Joe. You aren't misreading. I'm just . . . I need a little time."

"Not tonight, then?" he responded quickly. "Is that what you're saying?"

"I . . . didn't say that."

"Then what's wrong?"

"It's too fast."

"I have known . . . have felt this way since I first saw you, Marla. It's been weeks. That isn't fast."

"I've felt it, too. But I denied it until I saw you again. Until now."

Slowly he moved across the room. "Marla, I don't want this to be one-sided. I'm sure about me, but I want you to be sure, too. And no regrets. Two volunteers. Both willing or not at all."

She faced him squarely, a little smile playing around her lips. "This is crazy. You know I want you, too."

"Then why wait? Our time is limited, and it's slipping away."

She shrugged and laughed a little. "I can't think of any good reasons right now."

Joe closed the final space between them and took her in his arms. His fervent kiss was filled with promises of passion and tenderness, his body revealed the vitality of his desire. He raised his head and looked deep into her eyes. "Marla, we have each other. We're stranded on that island, alone... together. Just us two tonight. And for the next few weeks..."

Her arms crept around his shoulders, her fingers playing with the dark hair on the nape of his neck. "I volunteer..."

"Two volunteers," he murmured, kissing her again. Then he lifted her in his arms and bent to nibble her earlobe and bury kisses in her tawny hair. "God, I want to love you, Marla. To love you until you can't catch your breath."

"Promise?" She already felt breathless, even before he whisked her to the bedroom and placed her on the bed.

Her blond hair spread fanlike over the pillow, and he reached for the golden tresses while he rained kisses over her entire face. "Oh, woman, what you do to me..."

She slid her hands across the width of his broad chest, feeling the warmth beneath his shirt. "Show me," she taunted bravely and tackled the tiny pearl buttons keeping that shirt closed and his muscular chest from her touch. She felt desperate to see him undressed, to caress him intimately. Her slender fingers worked diligently until she reached his belt.

Abruptly she halted, suddenly aware that beneath his clothes Joe was hot and boldly aroused. Soon nothing would be hidden. And there would be no turning back.

"Don't stop," he encouraged and jerked the shirttail out of his waistband. With a flick of his wrist he unbuckled his belt and the waist of his slacks.

In another moment his shirt was gone and his broad, brown chest hovered over her. Lord, he was beautiful. So smooth and tempting. Spreading her fingers against him, she explored his skin's texture. "You've been in my fantasies since we first met, Joe."

"I want to see you, too, Marla. All of you. Then my fantasies can be completely acted out." He unbuttoned her blouse and helped her out of it. With feverish fingers he unsnapped the front closing of her bra and slowly released her breasts from their lace prison. Then he removed the rest of her clothes. His eyes flamed with dark fire as he looked at her, not touching but wanting to touch everything.

She lay back on the bed, smiling seductively. The hiss of his zipper told her what he was doing. Marla tried to keep her gaze trained on his but failed miserably. She was compelled to peruse his body, to address the awesomeness of his arousal, to look him over from broad, smooth chest to tight, brown hips. He was magnificent. And soon he would be hers to hold, to feel. Deep inside she ached to fulfill that long-dormant sexual yearning. When she lifted her gaze back to his face, she saw he was watching her.

Marla grinned sheepishly, suddenly embarrassed that he'd caught her admiring him.

"Well?"

"Beautiful," she said softly.

He moved closer. "Marla, are you . . ."

"On the pill? No."

"Then I'll take care of it." He scrambled for his discarded slacks, mumbling gruffly, "I know how this must look, but it's not what it seems."

"You expected us to get together."

"I hoped." He turned and moved beside her, their bare bodies only inches apart. "Oh, God, I hoped, Marla." He kissed her again, hovering but not letting their bodies touch. She could feel the heat of him, and it nearly drove her crazy. With one hand he swept down her length, fingertips brushing her breasts, past her waist, pausing to stroke each thigh until her legs relaxed. "Ahh, sexy," he murmured.

Smiling, she reached out to caress him softly. "I love the way you feel, Joe. So strong and wonderful . . ."

His skin rippled beneath her petting, and he groaned, forcing himself to be still and let her explore him with her feathery fingers. Joe's instincts commanded him to take her— and hurry—but he knew she needed time. And he also knew he should take it easy with her unless he wanted this time to be the last.

And he definitely didn't.

He turned to her, pulling her hands from him and placing them above her head. She gazed up at him, nude and wanting and willing. There was nothing to stop them now. Nothing to slow them down. They could go at their own pace.

At long last they came together, smooth and hard, thrusting and accepting. His kisses trailed from her neck to her legs; her hands caressed every muscle.

He nuzzled her breasts, his tongue stroking their rise and slope, circling their hardening peaks. He planted moist kisses along the heated valley of her cleavage, then laved each pink-crowned nipple with his tongue until it was a swollen pebble. As passion controlled her, she thrust her breasts upward, and he sucked each one until she moaned softly.

Marla had forgotten what such driving desire for a man was like. She writhed with the almost-unbearable pleasure of his lovemaking. She wanted him, urged him to come to her by arching her back, reaching up for him.

But he held her at the brink as long as he could stand it, skimming his large hand over her smoothness, the slight roundness of her tummy, her golden mound of pleasure. Fingertips feathered her inner thighs, then pressed them open. He could wait no longer!

Marla felt the weight of his large body sliding over her, between her legs. She responded to the pressure of his arousal and experienced joy as he entered her slowly, surely, completely.

They lay very still for a few moments, both relishing the sensations. Her hands stroked his back, trailed along his spine, cupped his buttocks, urged him farther into her.

Then he could be still no longer, and the rhythm he set was fast and furious. She met his thrusts with a force of her own, gripping his back muscles, digging her fingers into his skin for leverage. Spirals of uncontrolled zeal creating unimaginable pleasure swirled them to the highest peaks, enlivening their senses, sending them into a realm of their own.

"Joe!" she cried out again and again.

"I'm with you, baby. Every move." His response was a breathless moan. "Oh, God, Marla!" Then all was quiet except for their labored panting. They stayed like that, with arms and legs entwined, clinging to the rapture as long as possible.

When their breathing finally returned to normal and heartbeats slowed to a regular pace, he kissed her tenderly and rolled from atop her. After a quick trip to the bathroom he curled her to his body, hooking his arm around her waist.

Marla hadn't felt so content and fulfilled as a woman since she'd lost Wayne. With Joe the newness and exploring had been exciting. One of the wonderful things about Joe, she thought as she drifted into that hazy state before sleep, was his honesty. Even in his lovemaking. He had admitted his passion and acted on it. And she could no longer deny a woman's natural urge for a man's fulfillment.

During the night he held her securely in his arms, held her lovingly while they both slept. Content. Fulfilled. Loving.

When morning came, the autumn sun made a pattern on the Mexican tile. Joe sprawled, reaching for her with one arm. But her side of the bed was empty. He launched from the bed and quickly swept through the rooms, calling her name. Marla was gone. "What gives?" he muttered aloud. "Where the heck is she?"

Cursing, he thrust his legs into his discarded slacks, not bothering with underwear or his belt. On his way out the door he grabbed his shirt.

"I THOUGHT I'D FIND you here."

"It's so peaceful. Just the water and the rocks. And the sky." She sat on a jutting point of lava rock where the waves crashed high and sprayed the air with misty saltwater. They were a good mile from the casitas.

"And me. Been thinking?"

"Yes."

"About what? Or should I say who? Me?"

"Mmm-hmm. You and me."

"Want to talk?"

She stared into the distance over the water. "This was the first time since . . . since my husband."

Joe crawled across the uneven rocks and sat beside her. He took her hand and sandwiched it between both of his. Hers felt cold, and he wanted to wrap her up in his arms. "I was afraid of something like this. It seems unfair because it's beyond my power."

"Mine too. I'm sorry. I couldn't help leaving. I needed to think. Please understand it's nothing against you, Joe. The problem's within me."

"I just happen to be the one here?"

"There could have been no other, Joe. Not the way I feel."

"How *do* you feel?" Joe's sigh was heavy and audible. "Are you ready to let go of him, Marla?"

"I don't know."

"I won't compete with him. I'm selfish. I want you all to myself." His voice was low and strained with emotion. He didn't want to lose her now, especially because of something beyond his control. "But I can tell you exactly how I feel. I've never been so attracted to anyone as I have to you. I've never felt so sure about a relationship. And after last night—" he paused to kiss her palm "—I'm even more sure than ever."

"I appreciate what you're saying. And I'm grateful you feel this way because I do, too. Oh, Joe, it isn't you. It's me. I just . . ."

"Feel guilty."

"Yes."

"Don't do that to yourself. You're young, Marla. You can't stop living because your husband did."

"I know."

"You can't stop loving, either."

Love, Joe? Or lust? She didn't dare ask, but her expressive eyes revealed her doubts.

His response was low. "Marla, I only know that when I hold you, it's right. And last night was wonderful. No, the word's inadequate."

She smiled and agreed softly.

"I just want to know one thing from you, Marla. Any regrets?"

"No." She spoke with conviction. "No regrets."

"Isn't that enough for now?" he implored her. "I can show you happiness if you'll let me."

"I agree with your logic. I just wish it were that easy."

Joe took a deep breath. "I may regret this, but I think we'd better get it out in the open. Hiding and pretending doesn't work. Let's talk about him. What was his name?"

"Wayne."

"I really don't know anything about him. Was Wayne killed in an accident?"

"No. His death was the result of a rare virus that attacks the heart muscle. He became violently ill and died within two weeks. He was on life-support for—" She paused and blinked her eyes rapidly.

"This is too much for you." Joe felt his stomach knot as he listened to her pain. "You don't have to tell me."

"I want to. You're right. You should know. I should say it." She took a deep breath. "He was on life-support for the last few days and we finally realized . . . It became obvious that he wouldn't last."

Joe pressed her hand to his pounding heart. He wanted to take her in his arms, to hush her message with his lips, yet he couldn't. He could only listen to her tortured story. When she finished, his arm went around her shoulder and he pulled her to him.

She laid her head against the security of Joe's chest and listened to the rhythmic beating of his heart. It seemed to relate more than he'd been able to say. And words weren't required. His strength, his presence, his sincerity all combined to let her know his sentiment. Finally he spoke in a low voice. "I want you to know that I care about your feelings. And about you, Marla. But I won't intrude."

"You haven't, Joe."

He struggled to say the next words and even doubted for a moment that he could. "I'll walk away if that's what you really want. Until you're ready."

She sat up and looked at him in alarm. "Don't do that. Please don't leave me now, Joe." She leaned forward and kissed him. "I need you."

"I won't leave. I need you, too. Oh, Marla . . ." He groaned as their lips met again, and he hauled her closer. Whenever they touched, the magnetic powers between them were spontaneous. After only one night he couldn't imagine ever being without her again.

Finally he lifted her chin. "Let's go back, Marla."

She nodded and clutched his hand as they made their way down from the lava boulders.

"Here it is!" He pointed at a sandy slope between two rocks. "It's your perfect whelk!"

Putting their heads together, they examined an orange-toned shell. Suddenly it started to move.

"It has an occupant," she said, laughing. "A hermit crab is using it as his home."

"It's a beautiful shell. Looks perfect. Do you want it? We can get rid of that crab."

"No, he found it first. He—or she—deserves it." She slipped her hand into Joe's and smiled. "There'll be others. Anyway, I have about all the perfection I can handle right now."

He wrapped his arms around her and held her close to his warm body. "Oh, I don't know. I figure you're just about perfect, and I can't seem to get enough of you."

"See, it's not impossible to find perfection, if you look long enough. And you don't lose hope." She pressed herself against him, loving the way their bodies molded together. "Did I tell you last night was terrific, Joe?"

"About a dozen times." He chuckled. "I don't know if we're really perfect together, but damned close."

"Damned close," she repeated as his lips closed over hers.

7

"MY GOAL TODAY IS to beat you at tennis," Joe announced later after a meager breakfast of coffee and fruit with Marla. "Then chase you around the pool and—"

"Whoa! Don't I have anything to say about this?" Marla smiled at his enthusiasm. She knew he was trying to make her feel better after their rather melancholy experience on the beach earlier.

"Not much, unless you want to concede defeat now. With a breakfast like this, it's a wonder you don't collapse for lack of nourishment."

"It's plenty for me. You could have ordered more."

"No, I'm watching my waistline. Goes along with improving my image. Didn't you say cameras add ten pounds?"

"Sad fact," she said with a nod. "If we play tennis every day, I'm afraid we'll lose too much time, Joe. You realize, of course, that we have a lot of ground to cover."

He drew an imaginary line down her nose with his finger. "Wrong viewpoint. We won't lose anything. We'll gain by being together. And we won't play tennis every day." His finger traced her mouth, then he kissed her lips. "And we'll work later. Promise."

She settled into the comfortable circle of his arms. "You're very persuasive, you know."

"Smart girl. I knew you'd see it my way."

The few hours of sports worked as a boost to their budding relationship. The physical stimulation was good for their mental as well as physical well-being. It brought about laughter and relaxation and a more casual attitude of togetherness. She beat him soundly at tennis. But he outswam her by ten laps, at least. They ate a hearty lunch and raced back to the room. He won, being the runner, and teased her unmercifully when she stumbled into the room, gasping for air.

But when she caught her breath, Marla tantalized him until he soon became breathless, too. She fussed that he gave up too easily, but quickly forgot her objections when she ended up in his arms.

During the late afternoon they spent a few hours on communication preliminaries, such as listening to others and revealing oneself.

That night Joe lured her to his casita. Like new lovers who can't get enough of each other, they made love until they were exhausted and fell asleep nestled together like two spoons.

Breakfast the next day was a carnal affair, held in the middle of his king-size bed. She snuggled in her fluffy yellow robe. He wore only a towel around his waist.

Marla fed him guava-marmaladed muffins, daintily dabbing the corners of his mouth after each bite. Joe fed her *huevos rancheros*, eggs served on corn tortillas and topped with tomato-and-green-chili sauce, dribbling bits on her chin and chest.

"Aw, Joe, you're messy!"

"Sorry, I'll get that." He leaned close and lapped up every bit with his tongue. "Hmm, this is the part I like best!"

"You did that on purpose!" She giggled and grabbed a napkin.

He seized her wrist and pushed her back against the pillows. "Is there any other way? Hold still and I'll get it all." His kiss left no doubt about his interest in all of her.

"Breakfast is getting cold."

"But we're getting hot. Now which is more important?"

"Well, when you put it that way. . ." Her fingers traced the strong lines of his face.

"We only need to eat enough to keep up our strength," he murmured. "I can't get enough of you, pretty lady."

Slowly he stretched alongside her, not losing eye contact during the process. He moved closer until their lips touched and his tongue reached inside to the sweet moisture of her mouth. Her tongue met his, sparring playfully. With a low groan of pleasure he raised his head to gaze at her.

"When you look at me like that, I get butterflies inside, Joe."

"You with butterflies? Sorry, but I can't keep my eyes off you, Marla. You're a beautiful, sensuous woman. I still can't believe I'm really holding you and this isn't all a big dream."

"It's no dream, Joe. Touch me and see."

He swallowed hard and desire lit up his ebony eyes. Both hands stroked her tousled hair and framed her face, then moved down to the lapels of her robe. Slowly he pushed back both panels to find her alluringly nude. Releasing a pent-up breath, he voiced a guttural, "Beautiful . . . so sexy."

She smiled sensually at his obvious approval. "I never cared much for breakfast, anyway." She took his hand and kissed the palm and ran her tongue down its middle, then placed it over one breast.

He pressed both copper-brown hands against the soft pliancy of her creamy white breasts, the center of his palms against the prominent pink nipples and his fingers splayed against her bosom. Ever so gently he began to massage, generating a quickly mounting passion within her.

She writhed beneath his hot hands, then gasped for joy as he sprinkled kisses liberally over her breasts. Her skin tingled with delight, and she felt his breath in hot little spurts as his lips moved erotically over her. She couldn't get enough of his passionate display of affection.

"Oh, Joe, touch me everywhere." She wriggled in anticipation of his response to her command.

As his tongue created moist trails down her belly and to the sensitive area on her inner thighs, Marla felt aflame all over. She'd never known such strong passion, had never felt so alive when making love. She made soft purring noises as his hands teased her body, and gasped aloud when he pressed the centre of her womanhood. Long, firm strokes stimulated her to the brink of ecstasy, and her whispers urged him to finish what he'd started.

When he straddled her writhing body, the towel around his waist came off, revealing his full aroused glory. He paused long enough to make their lovemaking safe and she watched him, arching her back, encouraging him to hurry. Her hands were everywhere, assisting, tempting, begging.

When he was ready, she murmured, "Don't wait any longer, Joe...."

He slid his large hands beneath her hips and lifted her to meet him, his desire hard and vigorous as he drove into her softness. There was no holding back for either of them. He stroked her fully, slow and deliberate at first, then with a growing force beyond his control.

Joe knew that as a man, his first attraction to her had been her beauty. But now his feelings—not just his lust—for the lovely woman he was beginning to know were expressed in his physical lovemaking. He wanted her, wanted to satisfy his own sexual urges. But he also wanted to satisfy hers. And his need for her was rapidly going beyond sexual.

Marla vibrated with the impact of his body on hers, in hers. Looping her legs around his hips, she pulled herself tight around him, riding with each plunge to new peaks of pleasure. Her sexual needs seemed to match his, and she was consumed with only one thought, one frenzied act to be fulfilled. Her physical need was acute, her undulating motion tireless, as she moaned in ecstasy.

But in her heart Marla knew she couldn't be this free with any man, even one as sexy as Joe, unless her feelings went beyond the physical. He was a part of her heart as well as her body.

Suddenly Marla shuddered in a climax, taking him with her. A wild kind of joy exploded throughout her body, and she felt an emotional high that whisked her ever upward, swirling, whirling, floating in the rapture of a semiconscious heaven. For a moment she thought she'd cry with the surge of emotion. Desperate to retain the euphoria, she held on to him fiercely, murmuring, "Joe...my love...never so good..."

He wondered if she knew what she was saying. Deep inside he wished it were so. He knew he wanted her more each day and wanted his affection returned.

Finally he shifted, kissing her tenderly. "Unfortunately it can't last forever, my beauty."

"Too bad," she murmured and kissed his smooth, broad chest. "You and I seem to get better each time."

"Which proves the adage about practice." He chuckled as he rolled off Marla. They could hear dishes clinking, and Joe groaned. "I forgot about the breakfast tray."

"Nothing worse than cold eggs," she said with a chuckle. "Careful. Don't spill the coffee."

He moved his leg, then halted abruptly with a low curse.

"What's wrong?"

"I think I stuck my foot in the *huevos rancheros.*"

"That's worse!" She rolled over laughing, and continued chuckling as she helped him clean up the mess. Everything they did was wonderful and funny and full of delight. Even the second shower of the morning.

Later after she was dressed she made a fresh pot of coffee in the kitchenette and poured them each a steaming cupful. Soon Joe emerged from the bedroom dressed in white shorts and a red knit pullover. He looked fantastic and fit. And definitely more relaxed than she'd ever seen him. Marla wondered if she looked different, too. She only knew she was happier than in years.

"Ah, coffee's a great way to start the day." He inhaled before he sipped it. "After sex, that is!"

"Going out for breakfast?" She gave him a teasing grin.

"Nope, I'm perfectly satisfied." He gave her a pseudoserious glance. "I have another idea. Lunch." Standing, he gulped the coffee, then set the cup back on the table. "I'll be back within the hour."

"Joe, what are you up to now?"

"People to see, plans to make." He brushed her forehead with his lips, then decided on a lingering kiss on her lips before leaving.

When Joe returned, he discovered the note she'd left for him. Jogging next door, he found Marla huddled over papers and notes scattered over the kitchen table. "What's this? I leave your side for less than an hour and you go berserk."

"It's called work, Joe. We'll never get done if we don't get going."

"Right." He watched her impatiently for a few moments. "Uh, could we work on this later, Marla? Our rented boat and picnic lunch await."

"What?"

He pulled her to her feet and kissed her quickly. "Swimsuits and sunscreen. Everything else is taken care of."

MARLA TRUDGED behind Joe to the pier lugging a food basket and the flat briefcase she'd insisted on bringing. Joe carried a cooler full of iced drinks and a brightly colored Mexican blanket. He'd vowed to help her hunt for perfect shells on a different beach, and they'd agreed to launch the next phase of Speechcraft, which included her evaluation of him.

She smiled at his jaunty gait. He not only looked happy, but he also *walked* happily. It pleased her immensely to think she had something to do with that.

They piled everything into the motorboat Joe had rented. With a sense of adventure they left the security of the San Carlos Harbor, waving at the children playing outside little pastel houses along the way. They passed elegant villas built high on the cliffs overlooking the Sea of Cortez and private beach clubs designed to lure work-weary tourists. Finally Joe steered them to a deserted sandy beach almost hidden by rocky cliffs that jutted out into the sea.

When they reached shallow water, Marla stood up in the bow and shaded her eyes. In a strange combination both cacti and palm trees grew near the beach, and bright orange and blue bird-of-paradise flowers blossomed in proliferation. The whole place looked like a fantasy movie set, specially designed for a lovers' rendezvous. "What a beautiful spot, Joe! How in the world did you find it?"

"Talked to the right people," he said with a pleased grin. "Actually, I wanted an island for us, but there weren't any handy." He lifted her out, then hauled the boat up on the beach.

"Joe, you're absolutely amazing." She helped him unload the boat, then they left their things in a pile on the blanket and began exploring the tiny protected cove. It was a half-mile crescent of pure-white sand, bordered by rocky brown hills on one side and crystalline water on the other. Aside from the motor of an occasional fishing boat, the only sounds were waterfowl.

"They say when the tide comes in, it sometimes brings loads of shells. And they get trapped here because of those cliffs." He took her hand as they walked, lacing their fingers firmly, hating to let her get far away from him.

She liked to feel the power of his muscular arm entwined with hers, as if he could give her some of his strength. Occasionally the back of her hand brushed his bare leg, triggering erotic thoughts of those strong, masculine legs rubbing hers, seeking what she had to give. "I'll bet this place is magnificent after a storm," she said.

"Or during."

"You are adventurous, aren't you?"

"It seems to be protected here." He swept his hand in an arc to encompass the surrounding cliffs.

"Well, I, for one, wouldn't like to try it out."

He laughed. "You wouldn't like to hide out with me?"

"Hide out *safely*," she said. "I'm not much of a risk taker."

"You don't consider our being together a risk?"

"In what way?" She looked up at him questioning. Was falling in love with Joe risky? She hadn't considered it so. Maybe he meant risky for him.

"Oh . . . nothing."

"For you, Joe?"

"No, of course not." He'd answered firmly, but the seed of doubt had been planted and left them both wondering what kinds of risks they faced in the future.

They searched for perfect shells until the sand grew so hot that it stung their bare feet. Then they returned to their belongings.

Joe spread the blanket in the small amount of shade afforded by a palm tree. "I'd say we have three to four hours before the tide comes in, then we'd better scat."

"We can't stay here during high tide, and yet you wanted to ride out a storm?"

"Well, we couldn't do it here. We'd have to climb up in those rocks, maybe find a cave."

"A cave!" She shuddered. "You, me and the snakes!"

He pulled her into his arms. "I wouldn't risk hurting you, Marla. You're too precious to me." His tender kiss convinced her of his sincerity. "Now unless you want to give the shrimp boats a spectacular peep show, I suggest we tackle lunch."

"I agree." She wriggled out of his arms and opened the lunch basket the restaurant had prepared for them. "You hungry?"

"Starved. My breakfast was interrupted by a sudden heat wave."

She gave him a teasing punch and handed him a sandwich.

Later they swam and snorkled in the crystal-clear waters, then relaxed on the blanket with chilled wine coolers. Marla opened her leather briefcase and pulled out her notebook. "I think it's about time for work."

"You're diligent—I'll give you that."

"We have lots of area to cover and have barely begun."

"Are you hinting that you have a big job ahead to whip me into shape for office?"

She grinned. "Something like that. But it isn't an impossible job."

"Well, thanks. That really boosts my ego."

"I have other techniques in mind to boost your ego." She arched her eyebrows. "Anyway, that's not the area where you need help the most."

He lounged back on the brightly striped blanket. "Look at us, Marla. I'm relaxed for the first time in years. You've been good for me. And you...you're laughing out loud for the first time since I've met you."

She caressed his cheek with her palm. "You've been good for me, too, Joe. There was a time when I thought I'd never laugh again."

"Never is a long time not to laugh. Or to love."

Her dark eyes explored his. *Love, Joe?* "And now you give me both."

"Yes, both," he murmured as he pulled her down for a kiss.

When she raised her head, his dark eyes were smoky with passion. "Marla..."

"We have work to do," she reminded him gently. "So get comfy."

He brought several cushions from the boat and propped them against the tree trunk, then settled back. Marla sat cross-legged, her work in her lap. "Now let's see what you wrote about me." He peered at her notebook pages full of scribbled notes and read aloud, "'Tall, imposing, good first impression.' What about sexy?"

"Very," she said. "But I was reluctant to put that on paper."

"Hmm, maybe you're right. We ought to keep that between us."

"We need to discuss the value of good first impressions. It's very important in business and in politics. Statistics show people make assessments of others in about thirty seconds of the initial meeting."

"Thirty seconds, hmm? That's pretty quick. What kind of first impression did I make on you, Marla?"

She tried to sound nonchalant. "Good."

"Only good? What about spectacular?"

"Actually, that word's inadequate. I think I was curious about you."

"Weren't you scared when I knocked on your door at that hour of the night? Come on, be honest."

"No. When I saw your eyes, I knew you were trust-worthy."

"There goes my macho image. Shot to hell by the woman nearest to my heart! You want to know what I thought of you?"

"Not right now."

"Sexy," he persisted. "You had my attention immediately."

"Joe, you're getting off the subject."

"And when I saw *your* eyes," he continued dreamily, "I knew I wanted you. Right then and there. And something told me I would have you, too."

"You have a one-track mind."

"I just thought I'd let you know my first impression of Marla Eden. You weren't a little bit scared?"

"I was more than a little impressed. You had—have—a special aura; some call it charisma. Something that draws people to you. I think it's because you let people know you care. That's important when you're dealing with the public."

His hand touched her crown, caressing her hair gently. "I don't know about the public, but when we're together, Marla, I'm certainly drawn to you. Can't keep my hands off you." He twirled a blond strand around his finger.

"Let's try to stay on the subject, Joe."

"I thought we were talking about feelings."

"We're talking about *you*."

"I'd rather talk about you. How I love to make love to you."

"Joe, hush. Let's go on." She ran her finger along the page. "Where was I? Oh, yes, voice of authority. You have a very nice resonance to your voice, and it'll help convey that leadership quality you want."

"I do?"

"Yes, you do. We'll talk more about modulating your tone when we prepare for the video."

"Modulating? Like deejays do?"

"More or less. I'll show you how to keep your voice tone steady, mainly when under fire. You want to appear unflappable, even if you're excited or angry underneath. You must look and sound like you're in complete control."

"Aha! Never let them see you sweat!"

"Yes, that's it." She hesitated before proceeding. "That's the good part. Now for the zingers."

"Shoot. I can take anything. As long as you're the one delivering." He crossed his arms on his chest.

"Your body language is defensive," she observed softly.

Quickly he unfolded his arms and laced his fingers behind his head in a casual attitude. "How's this?"

"Well, it's an open stance. But I think you're overdoing it. Just let your arms rest naturally." She chuckled as he made a great effort to get comfortable.

"It isn't easy when you think about it."

"We'll work on that, too. Also, we'll concentrate on increasing your voice strength. There'll be times when you have to make three or four speeches a day, do an interview and engage in hand-shaking sessions that require constant verbal exchanges. And then there'll be times when the microphone doesn't work and you'll have to shout your speech to the entire auditorium."

"Okay, I need a stronger voice. Sounds reasonable. What else?"

"Most adults don't have natural stage presence. Some kids do, but most of us are intimidated when we walk onstage and face more than ten people watching our every move."

"Yeah, I'm sure I'll freeze right up."

"Well, I'll show you how to appear relaxed and give you some tips to remember. And next is something to do with communication. I call it intercultural communication." She paused and looked up. "For you, Joe, it's very important because you'll be communicating with and interacting between two cultures. Words, gestures, phrases and actions mean different things to different peoples. You need to be aware of those so you don't make a major goof in public."

"Hmm . . . keep the general statements innocuous?"

"Something like that." She nodded. "Last, we need to work on dealing with the media, both written, as in newspapers and magazines, and visual, as in TV and documentaries."

"Those areas, frankly, scare the hell out of me."

"That's why we're going to work hardest on them." She turned the page, and he could see it was barely written on. "Okay, remember we talked about your goals? Aside from what we've already discussed and what I mentioned today, do you have anything to add?"

He tugged on his lower lip while he pondered. "I don't intend to be an empty-headed speaker, one who has nothing to say. An old aunt used to tell stories of a great Apache leader who spoke to the wind and it carried his messages to the people in all the corners of the land. And when times were good, the people came together to feast and celebrate their good fortune. I'd like that to be my legacy, too."

"What beautiful imagery," she said softly. "I believe your speeches will be carried to the far reaches of the country, Joe. Maybe by the wind, but probably by the media."

He agreed solemnly. "You know, Marla, there is so much that I want to accomplish for my people." He knotted his fist and hit his thigh for emphasis. "That's why I accepted the challenge in the first place. I want to improve the quality of life on the reservation, not by changing it but by enhancing opportunities."

"I'm impressed with your ambitions, Joe. And I want to help you accomplish them." She had been scribbling furiously while he talked, then paused to gaze at him. She couldn't mask her admiration for the man, aside from her personal feelings for him. "Your future is so important for your people. I wonder if they realize what a gem they have."

"I don't know about that." He gave her a shy smile. "But I can't help feeling that I have a destiny, Marla. And I have to meet it." He rubbed the frown from her brow, then cupped her chin with his hand. "And you'll be a part of it."

"I wouldn't ever do anything to jeopardize your leadership, Joe." She caught her lower lip between her teeth. At some point they had to acknowledge their differences. That she wasn't an Indian and the impact of that on his leadership position would have to be faced.

He leaned forward and kissed her nose, his hand still cupping her face. "You won't, my blond beauty. You're going to make it all possible. I can't do a thing if I don't win this election. And I don't want to appear the bumbling fool in my efforts. I want my people to be proud of me."

"Oh, they will be. I'm sure of it." She grasped his hand and kissed his palm. "But we have lots of material to cover before I'll feel satisfied."

He leaned back and sighed. "You're right. We've played long enough. Tomorrow we start in earnest."

She nodded.

He fondled her hand, lacing the fingers with his and tracing the lines. "Did I ever tell you how much I enjoy just being with you, Marla? I'm convinced that we were meant to be together."

"I love being with you, too, Joe. You make me happier than I've been in years. But I—"

He squeezed her hand. "What?"

"I can't help wondering what will happen to us when we leave Mexico."

"We'll figure out something. I know one thing, Marla Eden. I can't be without you for long."

"I don't want to lose you, Joe," she whispered.

"Marla, don't you realize you've got me, body and soul?" He caressed her cheek with the side of his thumb. Then he pulled her down to him.

She rested her head on his chest. It was so easy, and almost clichéd, to say "You have me body and soul." Marla's feelings went much deeper and were much more difficult to sort through. She was afraid Joe Quintero had captured her heart, and that was harder to determine. And harder to admit. It had to do with love.

She still questioned the possibility of loving Joe after having loved Wayne so much. Was it true? Was it real? How could she forget Wayne? She'd tried to long ago and hadn't been able to. Now she was attempting to put Wayne in another part of her life, to keep him special, and letting Joe dominate the present. For dominate he did.

Her heart pounded a solemn beat that seemed to keep time with his. She couldn't help wondering about his destiny and how hers fitted into the scheme of things. How could their futures ever mesh, especially if they achieved their joint goal and Joe became the next Apache chairman?

He la... ha... zi... Chouta... ha da... wi... bat...
...m... ma... 'O... level if you pre... Smith i... oy...' i...
...ra... Maybe... he Co... ha... ai... that i...
support
...

8

As THEY'D AGREED, Marla and Joe dedicated the next week to intensive study and work. The warm days were spent covering mounds of information, with an occasional break for a brief swim, but there was no more idle time lounging on a remote beach. Marla kept a determined course, which Joe followed eagerly. They both felt the importance of his destiny. Soon others would be looking up to him, following his leadership. He had to be prepared.

The moonlit nights, however, were made for romance. They couldn't stay away from each other. Joe was an ardent lover, turning her on to pleasures she'd forgotten or never known. Marla reveled in his constant attention and returned the affection energetically.

They'd been working steadily Thursday morning in Joe's casita when he received a long-distance call. Marla stepped into the other room to give him privacy but noticed a light-hearted lilt to the conversation. Obviously it was someone with whom he was quite familiar.

When Joe hung up and sought her out, he wore a happy grin. "Little brother's coming down this weekend. His flight gets in Friday night. Maybe we should rent a boat and go deep-sea fishing on Saturday. Josh would love that."

"Sounds like a good idea."

"We plan to work on campaign strategy and goals. I wish you'd sit in on our brainstorming sessions. I'd like your input, Marla."

"Sure, if you really want me," Marla agreed, crossing her arms in an unconsciously defensive posture. "Joe, is my presence going to be embarrassing when your brother's here? I don't mind if you want to make everything seem strictly businesslike between us."

He glanced at her sharply. "Isn't there a hidden agenda in your words?"

"Hidden agenda? I guess you're learning something from my classes when you turn that knowledge on me. What I mean is, our whole affair has been pretty sudden, and I can understand if you'd rather keep it private for now."

"Josh is family. I don't keep anything from him. He's a big boy. He'll understand about us." Joe ambled into the kitchen and took a Coke from the refrigerator.

"So much for Josh. But what about others?"

Joe gestured with the Coke bottle. "Want something to drink? I think we have some Perrier, if you prefer."

"No, thanks."

Joe pried off the cap and tilted his head back for a large gulp. "Josh has his life; I have mine. We've never interfered with each other's."

She shook her head. "Joe, you're avoiding the subject."

"Isn't that what you taught me?"

"Actually, it's too obvious to work on me." She toyed with the corner of her notebook.

"What are we talking about here, Marla? You and me? Josh? Or the campaign? I merely asked you to sit in with us. You don't have to if you'd rather not be involved. I'll understand if you think it isn't your business, which technically it isn't. But you have such good ideas that I feel you'd be a great addition."

"You're sidestepping again. I think you've learned the skill of doublespeak, Mr. Quintero." She paused and took a seat in one of the living-room chairs. "But not from me."

He set the Coke on the table and approached her, bracing a hand on each armrest of her chair. He leaned toward her. "Let me make my meaning perfectly clear, Ms Eden. Forget the election and Josh and everything else except us. Personally, I want you all to myself. But since we don't live on a deserted island and must mingle with the rest of the world, I have to share you. I'm proud to have you by my side, Marla. And I'll never be ashamed of you."

"Do you really mean that, Joe?" she asked softly, a lump of emotion in her throat.

"Absolutely."

"I think you've learned how to project a voice of authority quite well."

He shifted downward to a more comfortable and intimate position, kneeling on one knee and resting his torso against her legs. "Weren't we working on body language when the phone rang? I have a few things to say on that subject." He leaned forward and kissed her briefly.

"We were still on power-talk."

His closeness sent her senses spinning and her papers askew. Her pen clattered to the tile floor when he framed her face with his hands and kissed her again. "How can you doubt me when the feelings between us are this strong?"

"I don't doubt you," she declared, touching his face.

"Don't ever—"

"Before we get carried away, Joe, we should review the delivery techniques," she managed to say, trying valiantly to keep their minds on the work at hand. "Can you remember the rules? What about volume?"

"Let's see . . . keep your voice even and relaxed." He shifted and let his hands trail down her arms. "How can I be relaxed when I'm so close to you?"

"Perhaps you should stand an arm's distance away. Now what about pitch?"

"Low and level. Actually, I'm feeling a little high right now." His hands reached hers and grasped them.

"And speed?"

"Take your time." He lifted one hand at a time to his lips and brushed them with slow, deliberate kisses.

"Breath?"

"Long breath, short sentences." He moved forward to kiss the wildly pulsating spot at the base of her throat. "I'm breathless at the moment. And a little hot."

"It's because you aren't breathing with your diaphragm," she answered, feeling equally breathless. "And rhythm?"

"My favorite part." He stroked the sides of her breasts. "Give a definite beat to the phrases."

"Musical, not physical."

"Yes, teacher." He kissed her again, rubbing his thumbs over her tautening nipples.

She tried to keep her voice steady. "And don't forget to enunciate clearly."

"Ummm. . .right." He mumbled something, then teased the corners of her mouth with his tongue. "Now on to body language?"

She brushed his hands from her breasts. "Don't fiddle. Makes you appear nervous."

"Spoilsport."

"Keep a poker face."

"We Indians are good at that."

"Don't laugh a lot."

"You mean I can't be joyous?"

"Not in public."

"Private's good enough for me."

"Keep an open body stance. Expand into space."

He chuckled. "I've got that one right now."

"Joe . . ."

"Wasn't there another rule about invading someone else's space?"

"Only when you want to appear dominating. I wasn't going to mention that one. I think you know it already."

"Another favorite." He took her hands and pulled her to her feet, ignoring the notebook and papers that scattered everywhere. "Let's go in the other room and practice breathing techniques."

"Joe, I don't think we should stop working yet."

"We'll hit on body language before lunch."

"Joe . . . Joe!" She laughed as he lifted her high in his arms and whirled them around. And into the bedroom.

WHEN THE PHONE RANG again later that afternoon, Joe reached for it, muttering something about it probably being Josh with a change of plans. But Marla could tell right away it wasn't Josh.

Joe replaced the receiver and turned to her with a tight-lipped expression. "Now how the hell did they find me here?"

"Who?"

"McAndrew and Company, developers from Phoenix."

"Developers of what?"

"Land. They work on large projects like shopping centers, office complexes and condos."

"Oh. What do they want with you?"

"I think I know. The man on the phone said he had someone who was anxious to meet me personally for drinks, to discuss our mutual business interest." Joe sat on the edge of the bed and rested his elbows on widespread knees. "Do you want to come along?"

"No, Joe. This is your business. It has nothing to do with me."

"I may need some help. You could pretend to be my secretary."

"That is definitely not my territory." She paused and looked at him. "You know what they're after, don't you?"

"Not exactly, but I have a good idea. A few years ago McAndrew approached the tribe with some deal about building various projects on the reservation. But an agreement was never reached," Joe explained without hesitation. "There was so much controversy and opposition within the tribe that the matter was eventually dropped.

"Last year another proposal was submitted from McAndrew. I understand it's different, but the goal is the same, I'm sure. To build something on the reservation. The tribal council tabled it until after the election."

"Smart move. That way the new chairman can be responsible." She sat upright. "If McAndrew knows, that explains why he wants to see you."

"No doubt." Joe rose and began to pace, resting his chin against one cupped palm. "I only know one thing for sure. The bottom line means profit for McAndrew, or he wouldn't bother. But frankly, I don't care about that. My main objective is to make sure that the tribe doesn't lose. If elected, I plan to assign a task force to study the matter."

"You don't want to reject McAndrew outright?"

"No—I don't know. I haven't read the complete proposal. How can I make a judgment on something I haven't studied in depth?"

"Then don't."

"Huh?"

"Don't make a decision. Sometimes no decision is the best decision. It buys the time you need." She scooted to the edge of her seat. "Remember when we listed goals and mentioned basic negotiating skills?"

"Yes." He snapped his fingers. "Great idea, Marla! I need them now."

"Now? On this short notice? You're meeting these people in only a few hours!"

"Just hit the high points. I'll get details later."

Marla scrambled up and began digging in her briefcase for another notebook, mumbling to herself. "You must think you can learn everything in one day."

"That's the general idea of a crash course."

She groaned aloud and pulled out the appropriate information.

"That's what I like about you, Marla." He gripped her shoulders affectionately. "You're extremely capable. And you either know a subject well or have the information at your fingertips."

"Thanks." She rolled her eyes. "Efficient is my middle name."

"It's just one of many fine qualities I like about you." He grinned and pulled her into his arms for a quick kiss. "We don't have time for a complete listing."

They spent the next few hours role-playing win-win and win-lose positions in negotiating. Marla focused on certain topics she thought he would need. Joe listened carefully, asking specific questions on some areas and dismissing extraneous details.

Finally he checked his watch. "Okay, that'll have to do for now."

"There's so much more."

"This will get me through tonight."

"Remember to focus on results, on what you can live with. Or, in your case, what you and the tribe would be willing to live with. Also, you don't need the developer's approval; therefore you have leverage."

He nodded. "I know where I stand."

"Good. You'll do fine."

He placed his hands on her shoulders. "Have I ever told you that you're terrific?"

"I just hope I've been of some help, Joe."

"You're all I need, my beauty." He kissed her quickly, then headed for the shower.

"You'd better hurry. I'll wait next door for you."

"I may be late."

"I don't care. Come over if you want to talk. But you don't have to, of course. It really isn't my business."

"I'll see you later," he called with conviction over the sound of the shower.

Marla returned to her casita, but close to the time for Joe to go to his meeting, she couldn't resist peeking out her window for a glimpse of him. Striding forward confidently, he wore a beige sport coat, open-necked shirt and navy slacks. Although dressed casually, he looked impressive. But then, to her he looked impressive in anything, with his broad shoulders and trim waist and dark, shaggy hair. Or in nothing.

His stride had somewhat of a swagger, a masculine holdover from his athlete days, she supposed. And he had a regal bearing, perhaps a trait from his ancestors. *He will make a handsome leader*, she conceded silently.

Joe disappeared beneath the arched doorway leading into the cantina. Marla turned around with a private smile. Just watching this man from afar did strange things to her insides. She'd never been so enthralled with a man, or so eager to love since her college days with Wayne. And even then it hadn't been the same. Their relationship seemed tame and immature compared to what she and Joe now shared.

She began to undress, thinking about the man she'd been sleeping with for a week. And how, in that brief time, her life, her enjoyment of life, had changed. Since she and Joe were older, perhaps they valued love and life more, whereas she and Wayne had taken everything for granted. Each other. Love. Supportive families. The possibility of kids. And yet over the years none of those elements had remained the same.

Wayne was gone and so was her father. Love was elusive; there had been no other. And having children...had been put on hold.

Marla let the last of her clothes drop to the floor and ran her hands over her firm breasts and down her slim middle. No love. No kids. She and Wayne had joked about having babies, but it had always been in the nebulous future.

But they'd been so young that it hadn't mattered. They would have plenty of time, they'd thought. Now he was gone and she was twenty-nine and counting. And still no kids. Of course she thought about it and went through almost-desperate periods of longing for a child, especially Wayne's child. She'd even considered adopting, but work always compensated or interfered. Or so she told herself.

Marla stepped into the shower and turned the water spray to massage. The rough water pelted her shoulders vigorously, stimulating intimate thoughts of Joe. He was such a good lover, but he also had many characteristics she valued. Joe Quintero was the only man since Wayne that she had considered being the father of her child.

This is foolish, she told herself. *We aren't anywhere near thinking about kids. We aren't even thinking beyond two more weeks in Mexico.* She considered what would happen to them.

Today Joe had said he would never be ashamed to have her by his side. She smiled, imagining him giving his acceptance speech after winning the election with her proudly by his side.

But first he had to win, he constantly reminded her.

She switched the shower off and began to towel-dry her hair. Her imagination was running overtime tonight. Back to reality. She wondered how Joe was faring with the developers from Phoenix.

TWO MEN WERE WAITING at the bar and rose the minute Joe stepped inside the decorative arch. They obviously knew him on sight. The slim one with glasses approached. "Joe, I'm Colin Hayden." He shook Joe's hand and steered him to his companion. "This is Mark McAndrew."

McAndrew was about fifty, a robust man with a sizable girth. He wore an expensive suede jacket that hung open for his midriff bulge and a diamond ring the size of a cat's paw on his fat finger. He extended a pudgy hand. "Mr. Quintero. Pleasure."

"Same here, Mr. McAndrew." Joe knew the stakes must have been high. The company's chief executive had come to play the game, and he wouldn't have made this trip to exchange pleasantries about the weather.

Hayden stood between them, smiling. "Gentlemen, how about a drink? And let's start off with first names, okay? It's so much friendlier." Hayden was apparently the designated spokesman whose first order of business was to reduce barriers, like the formality of names.

Both men nodded and let Colin steer them to a far table. The businessmen ordered highballs. Joe ordered a beer. He had no intention of losing any control this evening by drinking hard liquor.

Colin offered a toast when the drinks were delivered. "Here's to winning the election, Joe."

The three raised their glasses together, but there was no camaraderie. They were here on business and all were keenly aware of it. There was a bit of tension in the air.

Joe took a drink, set his glass on the table and waited. His body language said he was ready to listen.

"I understand you're the chosen one, Joe. They say the election is just a formality, a show of support," Colin began.

"That's not the way I view it," Joe countered. "I have an incumbent opponent."

"Ben Cartaro?" Colin scoffed and took a drink. "The man's a has-been. Too old. No new ideas. Not innovative. You're a shoo-in, man."

Joe remained calm but could feel his insides churning. "The election is a chance for choice," he said slowly. "I won't consider myself in until the ballots are counted."

Mark nodded. "Smart cookie."

"Very smart." Colin looked at his boss with trepidation, then proceeded. "I'm sure the costs of an election campaign are astronomical these days, Joe."

Joe nodded his agreement and narrowed his eyes. He could see what was coming.

Mark shifted his bulk closer. "So that's why we'd like to help."

"You came all the way to Mexico to contribute to my campaign, gentlemen?" Joe dug into his jacket pocket and produced a business card. "Contact my campaign manager. He takes care of the money."

Mark McAndrew grunted his disapproval, but Colin took the card. "Actually, Joe, we came to see you, face-to-face.

That's the way we like to do business. And we wanted to see if we could come to a meeting of the minds before things escalate for you."

Joe sipped his beer. "About what?"

"Ideas, Joe. Big bucks for your tribe," Mark injected.

Colin quickly explained. "We have a powerful proposition for the High Meadow Apache. It's the best kind of business deal where everybody benefits."

"Everybody?" Joe repeated.

"You, me, Mark, the Indians, everybody!" Colin waved his hand with growing enthusiasm. "Our plans will provide jobs for everyone. And something in it for us on the side."

"What plans?"

"Revised," Colin said sternly. "Plans for time-share condos on the reservation. We've had an architect design them to look like Indian cliff dwellings, you know? They're damned impressive, too. Real attractive. We'll put them up in the mountains at about seven or eight thousand feet and people from Phoenix and Tucson will flock up there, both summer and winter. Guaranteed eighty percent occupancy at all times. It'll be great! The profits are limitless."

Joe touched his glass but didn't drink. "Sounds too good to be true."

"Hell, no! We've got figures to prove it," Mark inserted. "It's legit, too."

Joe tried to keep his face expressionless, but the effort was increasingly difficult.

"We've got it all planned, right down to the engineering contract, which you would handle through your California company," Colin continued. "The Indians would be hired during construction, as much as possible. Then when the whole project is completed, there'll be more jobs."

"Like maintenance and cleaning?" Joe asked.

"Yeah, like that." Mark gestured and his large diamond flashed.

"All this and campaign contributions, too?"

"Hey, look, Joe," Colin said. "Somebody's got to build it and take the risk. We're willing to do that if you agree to work with your people."

"You mean, convince them to support your plan?"

"You'll have the power in your hands. You can do whatever you want," Mark said with a shrug.

Joe had had it. He slid his chair back and stood. "I'm sorry, gentlemen, this is one game I don't play."

Colin stood, too. "We've done our homework, Joe. It'll pay big. Don't turn your back on a sure thing. Play it smart."

A muscle in Joe's cheek twitched. His rage was barely controlled, but thanks to Marla's expert training, it was. "Your proposition stinks of bribery, and I'll have nothing to do with it. Or with you. This is one deal I can't live with, gentlemen. Thanks for the drink, but I have better things to do with my time tonight." He wheeled around and left the bar.

Colin watched him go, then sat back down and faced his boss. "It isn't over by a long shot, Mark. We've given him something to think about. And we'll be around. He knows we won't give up this easily."

Mark grumbled. "He's a damned fool."

"Naw. Just a little overcautious. He's new at the game. Give him time. Let him see how hard it is to get things done. Then he'll come running back."

JOE BURST into Marla's casita, rage darkening his face. "What do they take me for—a damned fool? If word of something like this got out, I'd be dead in the water. Did they really think I'd fall for the oldest scam in politics? You scratch our back, we'll scratch yours!"

Marla set her novel aside, surprised to see him back so soon. "What is it Joe? What in the world did they say to get you so angry?"

"They tried to bribe me! Campaign contribution, indeed!" He paced the length of the small living room like a caged lion.

"I can't believe they'd be so stupid."

Joe flexed his hands as if he'd like to punch something. Or someone.

Marla waited patiently until he cooled off a bit, not asking more than he'd readily blurted out.

Finally he sat down with her and fully explained their proposition. "Of course, I said no." He paused and looked at her with a slight grin. "Actually, what I said was, 'This is one deal I can't live with, gentlemen.' You would have been proud of my self-control, Marla."

"I'm glad you feel that something we worked on actually helped. But I'm always proud of you, Joe."

He grew serious and pressed his lips tightly together. "The hell of it, Marla, is that some of what they said may be right."

"What?"

"Jobs for my people. Jobs now and for the future." He sighed. "We're going to need businesses to do that. Businesses willing to take risks. I have to think about the total picture, what's good for the majority. What kind of future will my people have? Better job opportunities is one of my major goals. And what could be better than a large hiring operation on the reservation?"

"But not this way, Joe. I think you were right to refuse to discuss it further with these guys."

Marla watched as Joe's rage cooled. But the tension remained etched on his face. She knew this was just the beginning . . . the beginning of the end of their odyssey. Soon they would both be faced with the harshness of reality—the real world, not a make-believe haven in Mexico. She just prayed that reality wouldn't ruin their relationship.

9

"THAT'S 'LITTLE BROTHER'?" Marla gaped at the dark-haired hulk crossing the tarmac on the longest legs she'd ever seen. She hadn't expected someone *bigger* than Joe.

"Oh, I think he's only six-three. Or is it four?" Joe grinned and waved at the man who beat him by at least two inches.

When Josh had cleared Mexican customs, the two men grabbed each other like two sumo wrestlers, hugging and clapping each other on the back. Marla watched the rough display of affection and for a moment thought she might be out of place in this little family reunion. But Joe quickly pulled her to his side and introduced her with obvious pride.

There was a trace of family resemblance as sharp, ebony eyes quickly assessed her. Crazily she recalled the thirty seconds' first impression rule and couldn't help wondering what Josh was thinking of her. It was suddenly important.

When he smiled warmly and reached for her hand, however, Marla felt his unquestioning acceptance. "Hello, Marla. Nice to meet you." His attitude was genuine, and she felt better.

"Josh." Her hand was momentarily lost in his. "It's a pleasure. I've heard a lot about you."

"You mean my fame has preceded me? Joe, you said you'd keep the family secrets." Josh Quintero had an easy manner, not as serious as Joe's, and won Marla's heart immediately with his boyish smile and sense of humor.

"It was all good," she claimed with a grin.

"Ah, the consummate politician." He swung his arm around Joe's substantial shoulders. "Is this what she's teaching you, or your own idea?"

"It's too soon for the skeletons to come out," Joe said with a laugh. "You're looking good, little bro."

"You too," Josh said, standing back to reexamine Joe. "Better than ever, in fact."

"I *am* better than ever." Joe grinned at Marla.

Josh threw his head back and laughed. "Now that kind of vanity is definitely a Joe Quintero trait!" He turned to Marla. "Do you know he used to be a regular Joe Namath—he'd predict a win before a football game? Sometimes he would even stick his neck out and give a point spread—by seven or by ten. I thought he was bragging until he proved himself right a few times. After that I believed he could do anything he set his mind to."

"Now, Josh, don't bore the lady with old football stories!" Joe included her in the threesome as they headed out of the airport, laughing and talking and walking arm in arm.

Outside they stopped beside the yellow rented Volkswagen bug.

"You expect us to fold up into this little tin can?" Josh laughed sarcastically. "This is a big body, or didn't you ever notice?"

"Look, it's all I could get. Most people down here aren't linebackers with forty-eight-inch chests." Joe opened the door, and they gazed bleakly at the interior, which seemed to shrink before their eyes. "I had forgotten we were picking up the jolly green giant."

"I take offense to green!"

"Brown, then."

"And damned proud of it! Especially when my big bro gets to be the big cheese on the reservation."

"Gotta win the election first, little bro. And that's where you come in. We'll see if you're worth all those times I bailed you out of trouble and helped you limp through freshman English."

"Okay, guys. Enough! I'll take the back seat," Marla offered and tucked Josh's bag beneath her feet on the floor. "You two can squeeze into the front."

"Squeeze is right," Josh grumbled good-naturedly. "Now I know how a sardine feels."

The tiny car set the stage for more joking, and they drove to the beachfront villa in high spirits. Joe had made arrangements for Josh to stay in his casita. Marla knew it was the logical thing to do, but it meant they wouldn't be sleeping together while Josh was here. She admitted the two brothers had a lot of business to discuss and only one short weekend to do it. Somehow, though, it seemed like a very long time to Marla.

After dinner they sat in Joe's living room, chatting and drinking Corona beer. Sometimes the joy of being together erupted into a teasing wrestling match between the brothers, other times in an exchange of bawdy jokes. But all of it made Marla feel like a part of the family. Joe's family. It was a good feeling.

At one point Josh even brought up his pending divorce, and Marla knew she was accepted and trusted to be drawn into such a personal matter.

"You probably know I'm in the process of getting a divorce," Josh commented to Marla.

She nodded. "Joe mentioned it." She didn't want Josh to think they'd spent any length of time discussing him. In actuality, they hadn't.

"The lawyers are getting rich on this one." Josh had become tight-lipped and joking stopped. "I think it'll be drawn out because of the custody battle."

"How's Mick?"

"My four-year-old," Josh explained to Marla. "He's fine, I hope."

"He's with Judith?" Joe asked.

"On my lawyer's advice. I call frequently but sure do miss the kid." Signs of pain tinged Josh's dark eyes when he spoke of the broken marriage and his young son. "I'll be glad when it's over and we're settled into a family again."

Marla suspected this personal crisis was one reason Joe had asked Josh to be his campaign manager. It would certainly keep him busy during a difficult time.

Finally the conversation got around to the business of the election. Josh named the remote places around the thousands of acres of the Apache reservation he'd set for Joe to speak. "Most of those are in school auditoriums. One is prior to an art show in March. Also there are several media events in Albuquerque, Tucson and Phoenix."

"What media events?" Joe sat upright, mumbling, "I knew this was coming."

"TV appearances. You're going to be impressed with your campaign manager, Joe," Josh boasted with a proud smile. "With virtually no publicity we're already getting calls to schedule an appearance by the opposing candidate. We're going to keep you busy right up until the election, Joe."

"These are Anglo TV stations. Why do they want me?"

"Heck, this is the best way to reach more people, Joe. I've been working on this press release. See what you think." Josh drew a folded, wrinkled sheet from his pocket. It was well-worn and frayed.

Joe took the paper from Josh. "Innovative ideas . . . progressive programs . . . cultural renaissance." He looked at Josh.

"You fill in the blanks."

Joe ran his hand over his face and stared into space, thinking. "Okay, we'll work on it tomorrow."

"Sounds pretty good to me," Marla commented, reading over Joe's shoulder.

"Thank you, Marla," Josh said. "At least someone values my brilliance and expertise."

"Hell, Josh, it's great." Joe focused on the paper again. "It's exactly the format I want to state my platform. And I do have ideas about employment, education, enlarging recreational areas and hiring staff to oversee it—"

"Hold it, Joe." Josh grabbed a pen. "Maybe I should be writing some of this down."

"I like this part." Marla pointed to a line in bold print. "Joe Quintero, Apache, leader, man for the people."

Joe squinted at her. "Don't you think that's a little . . . overdone?"

Josh folded his arms over his chest. "Can you think of a better slogan?"

"No, but I haven't tried."

"Mmm-hmm. Well, we'll see what you come up with."

"Maybe Marla has some ideas." Joe turned to her.

She shrugged. "You are a man for the people, aren't you? Most of the programs you want to initiate are for the people."

Joe rubbed his chin. "Yes."

"Then why not say it?" Josh asked. "Tell them right up front what makes you different from your opponent. Already there's a great deal of outside interest in this election. The idea of the beloved incumbent, Ben Cartaro, versus the innovative businessman, Joe Quintero, has generated curiosity among the newspeople."

"Or they see a good, healthy conflict," Marla added.

"But can TV exposure affect *my* voters, the people I really care to reach?"

"The way I see it, the more exposure you get, the better." Josh leaned forward, elbows on his knees. His expression was earnest. "I think it's time to let everyone know what you're about, Joe. To increase respect. To let others know how the Apache are taking care of themselves. To bring attention to some of the problem areas where we need extra assistance. And to show that we're not the vicious savages they've read about in dime-store novels or seen on the movie screen."

"Wow, what a speech. You're really getting into this, aren't you, bro?"

"He's right, Joe," Marla agreed. "Maybe it's time to tell the world what you're about and how you plan to help your people. Anyway, if Ben Cartaro has been around awhile, everybody on the reservation knows him. But you're a virtual stranger to most. You need to be seen and heard to be understood. Do they all have TV sets, even in the remote areas?"

"Most do," Joe said. "Or some family member does."

Josh chuckled. "Or they could gather at the nearest trading post."

"The point is," Marla explained, "to let the voters know when and what station you'll be on, even if it's only a five-minute spot. Publicize your schedule everywhere—at the trading posts, in the papers, at every public function. That way the people you really want to reach will have the opportunity to see and hear you."

Joe had been nodding all along as she talked. "Sounds good."

"And think how convenient this will be." Josh framed Joe's face with his hands. "One trip to a radio or TV station and you'll reach thousands. By the magic of the tube, you'll be carried to the far corners of the land."

Joe and Marla exchanged smiles at Josh's reference to the old tale. "I told you you'd be speaking to the wind," she said softly.

"Have you been telling her Apache stories by night campfires, Joe?" Josh teased.

Joe reached for her hand and sandwiched it affectionately between his. "Afraid she knows all my secrets."

"And she's still around?" Josh gave her a big grin. "You're a brave lady."

"Like you, Josh, I believe in what Joe's doing. And I'll do everything I can to help."

"You're a smart lady, too. You've made some good points tonight, and I think Joe's on his way to winning an election. Now if only we could get the damned McAndrew project out of the way—"

"What do you mean?" Joe demanded.

"McAndrew has gone public with their condo proposal, claiming they're negotiating now with the Apache."

"Dammit!" Joe exploded and sprang off the sofa. "How could they do that? It's a lie!"

"They've just stretched the truth a bit, Joe. It's a technique to bring pressure on you and the tribe to make a decision, and to make it publicly," Marla said.

"I'll bet the tribal council is furious." Joe paced to the door, then whirled around. "Do they think I had anything to do with this?"

"They aren't terribly happy with the situation," Josh admitted. "You'll just have to let them know the truth, that you've had nothing to do with McAndrew."

There was a moment of silence before Joe spoke. "The truth is they were here last night."

"Who? The council?"

"McAndrew and his sidekick. They tried to bribe me."

"The hell you say!" Josh leaned forward, encouraging Joe to continue.

"They tried to get me to agree to use my considerable influence to sway the council in exchange for a sizable campaign donation."

"What'd you say?"

"Told them to go to hell!"

"They must have gone straight from here to the newspaper," Marla said.

"My, my." Josh clicked his tongue against his teeth. "Politics is such a dirty business!"

"This just emphasizes the importance of getting as much media coverage as you can, Joe," Marla said with conviction. "The people need to see and hear you in order to trust you."

Joe finally calmed down enough to take a seat beside her again. "I guess I do need to speak to the wind."

Marla laid her hand on his. "We have our work cut out for us, Joe."

Joe looked at her. "Yeah, we do."

An hour later he walked her back to her casita. "You're sure you don't want to go deep-sea fishing with us tomorrow?"

"No. You need to be alone with Josh. And I have no desire to spend my time catching fish."

"It's fun just to go out in the boat. You can relax in the sun and watch us fish. Water's clear and beautiful."

"I'll stick close to the beach this time."

"Looking for perfect whelks?"

"Yes, maybe." She sighed. "Maybe I'll find one this time. You never know."

He took her in his arms. "Josh likes you. He doesn't accept just anybody, you know. In fact, with his personal life so screwed up, he's been pretty miserable. Tonight he was more like his old rambunctious self."

"Well, with me there every second, he didn't have much choice except to like me."

"He's an honest man. It runs in the family."

She smiled. "You're lucky to have him so willing to help with your campaign. Now you two need some time together without me."

"I'll miss you." He kissed her deeply for a long time.

"I'll miss you, too," she whispered and finally slipped into her casita alone. This was ridiculous. She and Joe were acting as though they couldn't bear to be apart one day and a couple of nights. Yet soon they'd be leaving Mexico and each other. What would they do then? What *would* they do?

When Joe returned to his casita, Josh was gathering the beer bottles that had accumulated on the table. "She's a real beauty, Joe."

"Yep."

"And a very smart cookie."

"Agreed."

"I'm not blind. It looks serious between you two."

"About as serious as it gets."

"Great. Talk about complicating your life . . ."

"I know."

MARLA SPENT much of the following two days planning the next Speechcraft sessions she'd present to Joe. Occasionally she walked the beach alone, looking for shells, thinking.

At Joe's request she joined him and Josh as they made plans and discussed campaign strategy. She tried to keep her contributions to a minimum and not interfere or inflict her views into what she considered their domain.

When Josh flew out Sunday night, Marla was glad to see him go. But it was for purely selfish reasons. Now she had Joe all to herself. Suddenly she realized how very limited their time together was. And it seemed far too brief. She was in misery at the thought.

"He's great, Joe."

"Yeah. We got a lot accomplished toward campaign organization."

"And we managed to put together a pretty good press package."

"Thanks to your help." Joe tucked his arm around her shoulder. "Want to know a secret? I'm glad he's gone. Now I have you all to myself again." He nibbled her earlobe as they walked toward the little yellow bug.

Marla laughed. She felt better. Not so guilty at wanting Joe all to herself. Silently she thanked God their feelings were mutual.

THE NEXT TWO WEEKS went fast. They worked hard on creating a relaxed stage presence, looking cool when steaming inside and giving the media a good, solid story. They made numerous videos, played them, examined and changed every word, every nuance, every hand motion. Then they repeated the effort. The work was exhausting and time-consuming, leaving Marla and Joe less time to think about parting. But it was there, looming like a dark cloud on the horizon, creeping closer each day.

Their bodies seemed to radiate a certain glow, a white-hot light that grew in intensity when they were together. It was apparent in shining eyes as they sat across the table from each other in a restaurant. It kindled as fingers laced and palms matched when they held hands.

And when they undressed and their bodies came together, they ignited into a beautiful rainbow of color. The colors merged and blended and mixed with emotions and feelings, creating a collage of passion beyond conception. Beyond anything yet created, reaching beyond the realm of imagination. They were uniquely in love.

The night before they were to leave the resort, Marla and Joe embraced with a wild passion, a desperate clinging. He held her close, the heat from his bare body warming her through and through. Still, she felt a chill, wrenched from an icy core deep inside her.

She rested her head on his chest, her blond hair spread across the smooth coppery muscles. "It'll never be the same again, Joe. This has been so wonderful."

"I wish it could continue."

"So do I."

"What will you do when you get back home?"

"Spend about three days in the Phoenix office getting debriefed and catching up. My assistant, Kay, has been taking care of some of the more routine cases and local groups who've requested Speechcraft. But I have several people who've been placed on hold and are waiting for my return."

"Important lady. Everyone wants you, including me."

"What'll you do, Joe?"

"First, I'm flying back to California until after the holidays. My assistant, Kendra, is taking care of business, but...well, you know. I need to do some things myself. I think the real push of the campaign will start in January."

"Will you . . . come to see me when you're in Phoenix?"

"Of course. You know I will."

He stroked her back, his large hands caressing her bare length, framing her hips, cupping her buttocks. When he touched her, she felt alive, vibrant, yet strangely content. This was where she belonged, in his arms, resting against his strong body, responding to him in every way.

Joe pulled her over him, nestling her between his thighs. She felt the sinewy strength of his legs as he wrapped them around her. She rubbed her tight nipples over his chest, creating an erotic friction that elicited a small, low groan from him. Then the groan became her name as he arched toward her.

She reached up to caress his damp brow and his dark cheeks. He took in a sharp breath and she kissed his parted lips, giving him a taste of her tongue. She felt the warm power at the juncture of his legs expanding against her belly. Exciting and dynamic. Hot. She craved him with a sudden, intense wildness.

She wriggled within the vise of his legs, almost frantic to get free. "Let me go," she said with a gasp.

"Never."

"Joe, I want . . . you." She wedged a hand between them.

"Good, ahh, yes . . ."

When he loosened his hold on her, she slid upward to straddle him. His hands on her hips guided her to a glorious union. And all thought left her as she rose to the heights of ecstasy in a blaze of brilliance and color.

But somehow, through the haze of passion, his gasping words managed to reach her and register in her desire-veiled mind. "Marla . . . such love!"

In that moment they became one entity, one beautiful blending of colors, light and dark, love and desire, one. And the glow they created was as bright as Venus in a black winter sky. Finally she slumped against him and kissed a spot on his neck near his ear. "I . . . love . . . you . . ." she murmured.

He was silent and she knew he was dozing and hadn't heard her confession. And what would he have said if he *had* heard her? Probably nothing, for there was nothing either of them could do about it now.

Sighing, she slid from atop him to nestle in the curve of his body. With her back to his chest she felt him relax totally, knew the slow rhythm of his breathing when asleep. Inexplicably tears filled her eyes and spilled over onto her own breast. *Oh, how I love you, Joe.*

Although sleep was elusive, it eventually claimed her for a few hours. Early the next morning, while it was still dark, Marla slipped out of Joe's arms to walk the beach and talk to the waves. And to question why this was happening now, this way, with this particular man. Of all the inconvenient times, why now? Of all the inappropriate people, why him? Why couldn't their loving be easy?

There were no answers. No easy answers; no easy love.

WHEN JOE AWOKE and didn't find her, he didn't panic this time. He knew where she was. He dressed quickly and followed her at a jog, catching up before she reached the lava rocks at the point. Silently he took her hand, lacing their fingers. She smiled up at him, her face shadowed and strained.

"Look, I found a perfect whelk." She held it up for him to see.

"What? No brass trumpets? No band salutes? No wild applause?" He examined the shell with its brilliant color, unbleached and pointy edges unspoiled. "Very nice. How did this phenomenon happen?"

"I just looked down and there it was. Sometimes when you least expect it, you find what you were looking for all along."

"Sometimes when you least expect it, you find something or some*one* very beautiful." His ebony eyes were serious. "You're like that for me, Marla. You came to me in a time and place that I least expected. And you've become very special to me. I need you."

"Not anymore." Tears glistened in her big brown eyes, and her smile was tremulous. "I'm proud of you, Joe. You've absorbed everything I've taught, better than any other client. Honest. I'm convinced you'll do fine in the election. I'll look forward to seeing you on TV."

"Marla, I . . . you understand . . . there are . . . certain risks if it's known that I have an Anglo lover right now."

"I agree." She said the words with conviction, although her heart was falling apart. But he was right. "The private life of anyone running for election is up for such scrutiny these days that you have to be above reproach in everything. You know I would never do anything to jeopardize your winning the election, Joe."

"I want you to know that I don't intend for this to be the end of us, Marla."

"It's been wonderful. I'll never forget this . . . what we've had here in Mexico. But you have your job, your life. I have mine. I understand that."

"We'll work something out . . . sometime. I swear."

"Maybe another time we can meet in Mexico."

He took her in his arms and held her close to his heavy pounding heart. He had no idea their parting would feel this way, would hurt like this.

She pressed herself to him, wishing she could imprint him on her soul, afraid she would never get him back again. But she tried to convince herself of what they both had voiced.

"Oh, Joe . . . your destiny is foremost. It's greater than either of us. I believe it."

"Marla, I hate this part."

Her heart's pounding blended with his. "So do I."

10

THREE MONTHS LATER Marla sat before her TV set in Phoenix, hands clutched nervously in her lap. She was as jittery as a playwright on opening night. The performance wasn't hers, but she felt responsible for the show. And she cared about the critics' reviews—and the results. Lord, how she wanted Joe to do well.

In the past few weeks Joe had done several spots on the Phoenix noon news, and a couple of five-minute interviews in Tucson and Albuquerque. But this was the first time he'd made the Phoenix evening news. The big story was the proposed McAndrew condo project on the High Meadow Apache Reservation. When McAndrew and Company found that Joe wouldn't play the game their way, they had purposely muddied the political waters by making it one of the issues.

Neither Apache candidate fully endorsed or rejected McAndrew's proposal, although the incumbent was most critical. Joe's tactic had been to try to de-emphasize it, indicating that the Apache tribal council would study it and the people would eventually decide. It was accepted knowledge, however, that the economic future of the tribe might well be affected by the decision, and the news hounds refused to let it drop. This was McAndrew's real purpose of revealing it at this time.

Marla watched with pride as the camera moved in on Joe. His face was handsome and strong. Even the bright lights in the studio didn't diminish his copper complexion and the sharpness of his ebony eyes. His broad shoulders were squared in his navy jacket; the pale blue shirt and red tie completed the attire of a well-dressed businessman.

At her suggestion, he'd kept his dark hair slightly longer than the current mode, just barely edging his collar in the back. It gave him a somewhat rugged appearance, not too slick. She relaxed a little and admired him. Yes, the image was right and contrasted with that of the older incumbent.

When he spoke, Joe talked of the spirit of his people and how they would work together for the good of all. He tried to downplay the weight of a singular condo project by claiming there were other areas of equal importance, such as improved health care and education. His opponent had no real solutions but revealed distrust of outsiders' plans. When it was over, the camera moved back, showing both candidates. Joe looked strong, sure, secure.

Marla smiled and heaved a sigh of relief. He'd been magnificent, without a flaw. No spluttering, no uncomfortable gaps of silence, no negativism like his opponent. He'd relayed positive information, and he'd been good. Damned good.

She rose and flicked the TV off, then walked into the kitchen to finish making her chicken casserole. She prepared two salads and refrigerated them. She checked the table, already set with china, silver, wine goblets and candles on ecru linen with chocolate-colored napkins. The channeled whelk and several other "perfect" shells gathered in Mexico were piled stylishly in a basket as a centerpiece.

She nodded with approval. He would be here soon.

They might have a glass of wine on the patio if the weather permitted. They would eat slowly and talk about what had happened since they were last together. They would share their frustrations and joys.

Later they would retreat to her turquoise-and-beige bedroom and make love. Finally they would sleep, holding each other. And tomorrow he would leave. He had his busy world; she had hers. It had been this way since they'd returned from Mexico. Not very satisfying for either of them, but it was the way it had to be. For now.

JOE KNOCKED LIGHTLY and without hesitation inserted his key in the lock. He stepped inside and soft strands of Air Supply's "Now and Forever" drifted from the stereo. The candles were already lit, flickering a romantic welcome throughout the room. He paused and let the atmosphere surround him, engulf him, draw him in. For a few blissful hours he was transported to another world, Marla's world.

Yes, he thought. This was where he belonged. What had taken him so long to get here tonight? She was so good for him. She was what he needed, his refuge as well as his source of strength. He missed her terribly! He wished his life weren't so complicated.

Then she was there, in his arms, pressing her slender body to his, hands clutching his back beneath his coat, her face lifted, her lips slightly open, begging to be kissed. And his lips closed over hers, seeking their sweetness in an almost desperate fierceness.

When they finally parted, both were breathless.

"You're beautiful, Marla. I can hardly wait to see you each time."

"Sometimes the weeks go by so slowly without you, Joe."

"How are you? How's work?"

"Okay." She shrugged. "I've just missed you, that's all."

He shook his head. "I've been unbelievably busy."

"I know." She began sliding his coat off his tightly muscled shoulders. "I saw you tonight on TV."

"And..."

"You were..." She loosened his tie and unbuttoned the first
two buttons of his pale blue shirt.

"Yes, teacher?"

"Magnificent!" she whispered and kissed the warm pulse
spot on his neck.

"I had a good teacher." He lifted her chin with a finger and
kissed her lips. Then he planted kisses along her nose and on
the paper-thin skin of her closed eyelids. "Who is the perfect
lover. Do you know how much I enjoy coming here, Marla?
This place, and you, are like a little haven away from my
crazy, hectic world."

"I'm glad, Joe. I look forward to your coming so much."

"I'll be glad when this running around is all over."

Marla held the question *Then what?* on the tip of her
tongue. She didn't know what the future held for them. Joe
hadn't made a commitment, but neither had she. He couldn't
halt everything in his life and move to Phoenix. And she
couldn't imagine trailing after him on the campaign. They
had both agreed to keep their relationship private, at least
until after the election. Actually it gave them some time, time
they both needed to understand and sort out feelings and
emotions.

"I'll bet you're tired," she said gently. "Get comfortable,
and I'll pour us some wine."

In a few minutes she curled up beside him on the sofa and
snuggled into the curve of his arm. She rested against his solid
body, relishing his steely strength. They sipped their wine
quietly and listened to the words of Air Supply's "Even the
Nights Are Better."

He turned to her, sliding his hand beneath the silken weight of her hair. It looked golden in the soft light. "These nights with you are better than I ever dreamed they could be." His lips brushed her ear with sexy whispers as he kissed her temple, then her cheek. "Hmm, you smell delicious . . . taste fantastic."

He nibbled sweet moist kisses over her face and lips. She closed her eyes and let his kisses take her away, away to ecstasy. Just being with him, feeling him next to her, lifted her spirits and renewed her hopes that someday they would be able to live like this every day. Every night. A routine of beginning and ending each day together sounded heavenly but seemed remote at the present.

Joe shifted away from her and lay back with a heavy sigh. He reclined his head on the sofa, stretched his long legs out and propped his feet on a cushioned stool. Then he took her wineglass and set it on the side table and pulled her head gently down to his lap. "Closer," he mumbled.

She rested on the sinewy cushion of his thigh and listened to the next song on the tape, "Taking a Chance on Love." She couldn't help wondering if that's what she was doing, taking a chance with her heart. But she was helpless to change a thing.

When Joe touched her, though, and held her in his arms, Marla was convinced there were no risks for her heart. He had to feel the same as she did or he couldn't react to her so positively. And he wouldn't still be finding time for her in the midst of his hectic schedule. Like tonight.

He moved one hand caressingly over the curls at her forehead and temple. It was soothing, yet sensuous. He let his other hand rest on her rib cage. Occasionally he stroked her breast, as if to reacquaint himself with her softness, her femininity. The unobtrusive motion was quietly erotic and alerted her senses that more would follow.

"This McAndrew thing is getting more complicated," he said finally.

"I know the media is trying to play it up. You handled it well tonight, saying other areas are important, too."

"Well, they are. I really believe that without proper health care, improved facilities and skilled professionals, my people's health will decline. We have some specific problems that I intend to address when I'm in office. And I feel strongly that education is the key to the future. We have to improve that, as well."

"Nobody could argue with those points. They're pretty general."

"But I can't deny the importance of economic development for my people, particularly on the reservation. And McAndrew is offering a tempting opportunity. It looks good on the surface."

"What about beneath the surface, when you dig deeper?"

"Problems. Good and bad. Pros and cons."

"What are they? List them, Joe. Sometimes it helps to write them out, look at them, study them. Weigh them."

He sighed and began to recite what he'd reviewed in his mind numerous times. "First, the pros. They'll provide jobs for my people. Good jobs. They'll be hiring construction workers, large equipment operators, bricklayers, electricians, carpenters, interior finishers and designers, everything that goes with building a large project. Even engineers."

"So they claim."

"We'd cover it by contract to make sure they hired Apache first and foremost."

"Good point."

"Then when the project's finished, there would be other jobs available for locals. Maintenance, cleaning, possibly even lower-level administration."

"Sounds pretty good so far, Joe."

"Yep." He sighed and curved his hand around her face. "And I'm not denying that we need those jobs. Damned bad."

"Okay, what are the cons?"

"We'll have a major business on our reservation over which we won't have complete authority. There are potential problems in the future with something so large and so long lasting that we don't own. My people are disturbed by that. You can't blame them for wanting controlling interest in any large industry located on the reservation."

"Perhaps the tribe could buy them out eventually."

"It's possible, I suppose. But that's still questionable. It would take an amount of money the tribe doesn't have right now and may not have in the future. Anyway, that's a highly doubtful speculation. What if McAndrew doesn't want to sell? Or circumstances and policies change? We could do nothing about it except take him to court—another expensive endeavor."

"Even though it isn't likely, it's always possible."

He caressed her cheek. "So why set ourselves up for potential problems? The other major objection is that McAndrew insists these condos be built in the high country. The forests are thicker, making the entire site more appealing. The views are doubly spectacular, and the commercial possibilities of promotion and marketing will be greater."

"He's probably right. Is this on presently undeveloped land?" She caught his wrist and moved his palm over her mouth so she could kiss it.

"Uninhabited by humans. But the tall trees, high in the mountains, are the nesting grounds of the bald eagles. You know what importance the Apache place on the eagle. Building anywhere in the area could drive the birds away. Or eventually destroy them completely. My people are disturbed about this."

"I can understand why." Marla thought of the great bald eagle, extinct in much of its former habitat in the U.S. How beautiful and majestic it was in flight. She also knew the Apache used the bird's feathers in certain ceremonies, so it had religious significance.

Joe continued. "On the other hand, should the future and potential of people be pushed aside for the welfare of a creature? Is a bird, even a rare one, more important than people's needs?"

"You aren't asking me to answer that, are you?"

"No. Of course not. I'm mulling all the possibilities and options over in my mind. And I appreciate your listening. Actually, there are no easy answers here, and I don't expect you to come up with any. There are definite pros and cons; and there are strong reasons to consider this project, even though I personally reject McAndrew's approach and methods."

"Then it isn't all bad."

"No, nor all good. The bottom line is what's best for my people. And a decision won't be made finally until after the election. It will be a joint decision and eventually be put to a vote, but people are looking to me to lead them in the best direction."

"I'm sure you'll figure out what's best for your people, Joe."

"Marla . . ." He touched her breast, then slipped his hand beneath the thin material of her wraparound dress. The soft mound grew taut, the nipple button hard. He rubbed his palm across the pebbly tip, then sought her other breast. When it, too, responded, he whispered, "Marla, what's best for me is you. Make love to me."

Eagerly she led him to the bedroom and quickly undressed him, caressing, stroking, kissing. Seductively she dropped her dress and panties at her feet, undulating her hips as she joined him on the bed.

Joe lay back, thoroughly enjoying Marla's sexual aggressiveness. She kissed his lips and chin and chest, letting her tongue trail sexily over him and travel lower to his flat belly. Joe found that it was all he could do to remain still as she continued her maddening advances.

Finally she lowered herself over him until they were joined intimately. Sensuous, heated, breathing strong, passionate, hotly pressed together, touching, caressing, loving, softly murmuring.

Suddenly the fervor that drove them together increased in intensity, and he surged with an almost uncontrolled speed and force. She received him with a responsive, erotic eagerness. They rocked, matching thrust for thrust, in a wild fury. Passion swirled them in a fierce, voracious frenzy and slowed only when they climaxed and she slumped into his arms.

She awakened to his tenderly stroking hand. "Marla, I'll be so glad when this whole thing is over, and we can be together all the time."

"Will we?"

He stared at the ceiling. "We'll figure out a way."

"I hope so, Joe," she whispered and started to get up.

But he reached out and pulled her to him. "Don't go yet," he whispered.

Marla rested her head on his chest, pressing her knees together, trying to retain the feelings of having the most intimate part of Joe within her. And she knew she was trying desperately to hold on to him, to eliminate the fear she would lose him in the end.

Joe felt relaxed and sated. He relished their physical relationship; it was good and satisfying. But it wasn't enough. Not now. Sex was fleeting. He wanted her with him all the time.

His stomach growled and she chuckled. "Anybody hungry? I have a wonderful casserole all warm and waiting."

"Sounds sensuous to me."

"Could be."

"Then let's try it."

"I knew you couldn't refuse sex or food."

He patted her lightly on her derriere. "Not if you're serving up the feast, my love."

Marla smiled and held his last words in her heart.

THE NEXT MORNING Joe was already awake and having coffee when Marla's eyes popped open. It was later than her usual rising time. As she padded through the living room in her old yellow robe and matching scuffs, she noticed a sheet of paper with lists of pros and cons lying on the coffee table. She knew he'd been up early stewing over his decisions.

Joe kissed her and teased her about sleeping in. "Coffee for the princess? And what would you like for brunch? I'm cooking."

"Oh? Wonderful." She considered her options, given her stock and supplies. Looking at him with a perky smile, she suggested, "How about a Belgian waffle topped with fruit and a rasher of bacon on the side?"

He put his hands on his hips and eyed her. "You think I can't, huh? Where's the waffle iron? And the bacon?"

With a sweep of grandeur in her frumpy robe, Marla showed him the utensils and ingredients. Then she took her steaming cup of coffee to the table where she sat watching him, thinking how magnificent he looked puttering around her kitchen.

He placed bacon slices on a slotted microwave dish, covered them with a paper towel, then looked at her questioningly.

"High. Eight minutes," she responded automatically.

"Marla, I've been thinking—"

"I assume that's why you were up so early."

"What else could I do while you were sleeping?" He closed the door of the microwave, then turned his attention to the waffle iron, swiping the indented griddle with a brush dipped in corn oil.

She curled a leg under her. "Did I give you enough quiet time to think it through?" She held her breath. Could he have been figuring out a way for them to resolve their own personal crisis?

"Maybe. It involves our options with the McAndrew project." He dumped a cup of pancake mix into a bowl.

She hid her disappointment when he revealed his preoccupation with tribal crises. It was the reality she had always dealt with and would in the future if he were elected. Suddenly she gasped and started to rise to his assistance as he cracked an egg on the side of the bowl and it slid onto the cabinet instead of into its intended destination.

"I'll take care of it." He held her off with one hand upraised, and a few dozen curses later, he'd cleaned up his mess and started again with another egg. This one went into the bowl. He gave her a self-satisfied smile.

She chuckled and her brown eyes crinkled at the corners. How she loved having him around. "Well done. Carry on."

"Where was I? Oh, yes. I remember in the negotiating techniques you taught me that one commitment response is 'I like it,' which doesn't always mean yes."

She nodded. "Sometimes it's just a delaying tactic."

"Then there's no, which I'm not prepared to make yet," he continued. "Then there's the classic 'I'll let you know later.' Which is another, more honest, delaying tactic."

"Right. Another good delay is to ask for more clarification or information so you can make an informed decision."

He poured the batter into the center of the hot griddle and it sizzled as he closed the top. "I've used all of those so far. And McAndrew knows there will be no decision from either candidate until after the election, so he's not pushing."

"Just keeping the pressure on," she muttered.

"As if I don't have enough right now." He filled another cup of coffee for himself and warmed hers, then joined her at the table. "But I'd like to use this time to evaluate everything and try to come up with some solutions."

"Actually there's no rush, Joe. The more time you have, the better it will be for your people in the long run."

"The other negotiating response is to make a counteroffer, a trade-off." He paused to drink his coffee.

She leaned forward on her elbows. "Do you have something in mind, Joe?"

"I'm still working on it. The way I look at it, McAndrew's deal isn't great for the people, but it beats nothing. To refuse when there aren't enough jobs could mean no future economic gains for the reservation and the people will suffer, perhaps more than if we'd agreed to the condos. My counteroffer, then, could be along the lines of—"

A wisp of gray smoke drifted toward the ceiling behind him.

"Joe! You're burning the waffle!" Marla jumped up and rescued the charred creation. She dumped it in the sink and turned around with arms folded across her chest. "I'll fix breakfast. How about Cheerios?"

"Yeah, yeah, anything. Sorry about the mess. I'll help clean it up later." He took his coffee out onto the patio.

"Sure, later. Obviously you can't think and cook at the same time!" she yelled after him.

He poked his head back in the door. "No, but did I ever tell you you're terrific?"

"Are you going to finish that conversation? I'm dying to know!"

"Later. Gotta think about it some more."

"Joe!"

"Thanks for letting me bounce ideas around."

"It's called therapy. I'll send my bill next month."

"I could never repay you."

She looked up and caught his wicked wink. Then he hunched over the patio railing, sipping coffee, his mind a thousand miles away from her.

Only love me, Joe. That's all I ask.

11

"LISTEN TO ME, Josh. If we don't come up with an alternative, we'll be fair game for McAndrew." Joe's fist pounded the round table and scattered an assortment of papers and notes.

The small conference table where Joe and Josh had spent many hours brainstorming almost filled the tiny office in the High Meadow Tribal Building. The council had provided him the space until the election, when he'd either have the chairman's roomy office at the other end of the building or be heading back to California.

"I'm afraid that's the way he views us, anyway," Josh admitted honestly. "McAndrew's got the upper hand because he's got the money and the plan."

"That's even more reason we need a plan of our own," Joe countered stubbornly. "I've talked to enough people. I know they'll reject this proposal. Then we all may lose."

"Frankly, I feel they should reject it." Josh folded his arms across his substantial chest. "Nobody should develop that area to the north and risk destroying the eagles' nests. Can you imagine the field day the environmentalists would have with that one?"

"I agree. But more, I believe strongly that the Apache should have control of any major projects on the reservation. This is the wish of the people and we have to listen. To go against them invites even more trouble."

"Yep, no ownership means no control."

"Believe me, McAndrew's shrewd." Joe waggled his finger for emphasis. "I've met the man and he's after a profit. He sees this area as fertile ground."

"I suppose from a business standpoint, it is. We have eager people and substantial amounts of undeveloped land. We need jobs. All that spells opportunity."

"Yeah. He makes his living taking advantage of such opportunities. And he's good at it. McAndrew will come up with something else, if this deal doesn't fly. If we can't fill this potential economic void, he will. He'll . . . move the project away from the eagles or . . . or—"

Josh snapped his fingers. "Maybe that's a start for us. Move the project."

"Move it? Why not cancel it? The idea smacks of mercenaries, high-profit vultures. Time-share condos on an Indian reservation?" Joe winced. "Sounds so . . . damned commercial. His plan would draw only the wealthy, people who have excess money and time. Now how could our people relate to that kind of life-style?"

"McAndrew's claim is that guests would be spending money on the reservation. What's wrong with that?"

"What's wrong?" Joe shook his head. "There isn't enough creativity and input from us. It's a one-sided business with no incentives for our people. No ongoing endeavors with room to grow and change. No entrepreneurship."

"My God, Joe. What do you expect? You want everything!"

"You bet I do. But it's for our people. I believe they should be in charge of their own destiny. We shouldn't be shoved around by outsiders anymore."

"So you're saying the solution has to come from inside."

"Damned right. I believe it."

"And what if we don't have the skills to do it? What if we try something and fail?"

Joe spread his hands. "Then we fail. But we can't blame anyone else for it. We learn from failure and try again. It just has to be that way, Josh."

"Okay, so you want some kind of building project, but something not so big and commercial as time-share condos?"

"Big doesn't bother me. Nor does commercial, frankly. Realistically we're probably going to need something expansive to create the kinds and numbers of jobs we want."

Josh held up one hand, palm out, as if in warning. "We're talking about substantial start-up funds here that we don't have. But if we planned a large project in stages, created part of it and got it working—"

"Then used the functioning part as collateral to acquire funds for the next stage . . ." Joe interrupted with a growing eagerness. "And that way there'd be no huge rush to get the damned thing functioning in a year or two. It could be a long-term project, ongoing and meeting the needs of the people all along by providing jobs and opportunities."

Josh shrugged. "It could even change over the course of time, if the people decide it isn't functional for them anymore."

"Now we're rolling. I like that. Do it in stages. Something for the people, something they control, yet make it profitable."

Josh whipped out a clean sheet of paper. These notes would join the reams already accumulated from various brainstorming sessions. "Okay, what have we got here? Are condos out?"

"Yeah, condos are out. But I'm not opposed to apartments. Hold it. We're getting ahead of ourselves. That's later.

First we need..." Joe pushed himself away from the table and walked to the window. He shoved his hands in his pockets and stood there quietly for a few moments. "What I'd like to see first . . ."

"Come on, big brother. Spit it out. What's in that head of yours?"

Joe turned around, his expression uncertain as he tested his idea on Josh. "I've always wanted to see a cultural arts center on the reservation. A big building that could house a variety of Native American activities, especially Apache crafts and arts."

"You mean, something like a museum?"

"A *living* museum," Joe said with a little rush. "People could gather on the premises to do their work, to exhibit and show, to sell, to interact and participate in joint projects. Even to dance or hold ceremonies. It would be a place for the people. And possibly outsiders could attend for a fee, the way they do at any other museum."

"A living museum," Josh mumbled, mulling the idea over in his mind. "I like it. Like it a lot. Have you mentioned it to anyone else?"

"I bounced the concept off Uncle Will once when we were fishing."

"And? What was his reaction?"

"Said he wasn't sure. Needed time to think about it."

"That could take years," Josh said with a shake of his head.

"But I got a more immediate response when I talked with Aunt Minnie and her friend, Rose. They make miniature burden baskets together and sell them in shops in Phoenix and Tucson, so they know about the commercial market. And the difficulties involved. They liked the idea and even suggested building a heritage room where ancient Indian crafts could be taught and practiced. That way the arts would never die."

"Hey, yes. Great idea!" Josh made more notes. "Did you tell any others?"

Joe shook his head. "Just you."

"It's a damned good idea, Joe. So far, the count's running four in favor and one undecided. Not bad for something that has no real plan yet."

"But it has a purpose for our people. And that's what counts. A purpose."

"Yeah, Joe. I agree." Josh took another sheet and began scribbling. "Okay, we have a cultural center to be built first with possible apartments in the future. What about accommodations for tourists once they get here? The reservation's not the center of a metropolis, you know. There's no McDonald's or Holiday Inn on the corner."

"You mean . . . restaurants and hotels? We do need them, don't we?"

"Yeah, if you plan to bring people in here, you have to provide for them. There may even be a market for a variety of shops. Maybe a whole bunch in a complex—"

"That's it, Josh!" Joe's expression became animated as the ideas flowed freely between them. "A total Indian complex. Something that will take planning, architectural studies, engineering—not necessarily my company, though—we'll bid it out. We'll employ Indians as much as possible. Otherwise, we'll hire from the Anglo community, but it'll be on a job-by-job basis. We'll retain control."

"We'll need to get professionals to design it. Can we find enough from the Indian community?"

"I'm sure we can, if we start looking," Joe said. "For instance, I know of an Apache architect in Phoenix."

Josh's excitement grew along with Joe's. "I think we're on to something big."

"Indians will be a part of every step and stage, both professional and nonprofessional. Young and old, skilled or untrained. We'll train them, teach them skills, make jobs available. This is *it*, Josh!"

"You know what else we can do?" Josh leaned back and tapped his cheek with a finger. "Federal grant monies are available to Indian businesses. We just need to apply properly in order to receive the funds."

"We'll get a lawyer to look into that a.s.a.p." Joe walked to the huge map of the reservation tacked to the wall. "Let's see now. Where would be some possible locations for something of this magnitude?"

Josh stood behind him, then pointed. "This area is the most logical. It's land that's already cleared, already has roads. You've got to admit it's very scenic."

"But it's already in use."

"Just vacation homes."

"The residents have paid for land leases. Some Apache live on this side." Joe moved to another section.

"Compare the profits of the vacationers versus this multimillion-dollar project."

"Well, I'm not sure it's profitable at all right now. It's self-sustaining, though. Maybe if we cut garbage and sewer services, profits could be increased." Joe shrugged and tried nonchalantly to steer Josh's attention away from the lake, but his campaign manager seemed single-minded about it.

"Why don't we do a feasibility study? I would certainly expect this Indian center to be highly profitable in the long run. As well as something of the people, for the people."

"Yes, oh, yes." Joe's lips pressed together, and he could feel a tightening in his chest. A study would commit the fiscal facts to paper and eliminate any sympathetic views.

"Another thing," Josh continued. "If we use this area that's already available, we won't have to clear new land. That should please the environmentalists and the Indians."

"But it isn't available, Josh."

"It could be easily enough."

Joe shook his head. "Not easily at all."

"But it's recreational land and most of the inhabitants are part-timers."

"They own land leases."

"End the leases when they come up for renewal."

"Dammit, Josh—" Joe ran his hand around the back of his neck "—we can't!"

"Why not? It would take some adjustment, but—"

"Adjustment! It would take eviction!"

"Think of the total picture." Josh stared at his brother. "What's wrong with you? Suddenly you're being unreasonable. This sort of thing is done all the time, Joe, when new and better use of the land is needed."

"My God, Josh," Joe muttered hoarsely. "This would hurt Marla more than anything I could possibly do!"

"How?"

"She owns one of the vacation houses. Her father built it. There's a great deal of sentiment attached to the place."

"Now I understand your resistance, Joe." Josh shuffled across the room and took his seat again. All was quiet for a minute. Then he took another tack. "But you're dealing with this from a strictly personal level. I'm thinking of what's best for the whole tribe." Josh looked at his brother and saw the anguish on his face. "Sorry, bro."

"You're right." Joe's tone was hollow as he walked to the door. "Call a meeting with Albert and John and Phillip. Also Uncle Will and any others you think should be in on this. We need to talk. And plan."

"Where are you going?"

"I'll be back later. I need to think."

"Joe, are you—"

"No, I won't fight it. I'll go with the majority, after a feasibility study. And when I'm assured there is no other—better—location." He walked out of the building, feeling the tremendous burden of a leader. A good leader had to consider what was best for all, not best for any one person, even if that one person meant more to him than anyone else.

Joe Quintero was a man with a heavy heart. He could only imagine what this developing project would do to Marla as he drove Uncle Will's truck into the mountains. He went as far as the end of the pavement, then parked and walked along the dirt road. He'd already planned to buy a Jeep if he won the election. Living on the reservation almost required a four-wheel-drive vehicle in the winter. But he also wanted to be able to travel for pleasure in the rugged high country. Knowing Marla, he was sure she'd want to, also.

He breathed deeply, thinking how Marla would love this. The heavy pine smells, the moist air, the special feelings of being in a remote place and seeing wild animals. Joe wanted to bring her here, to this place of his ancestors . . . near the home of the mountain spirits and the wind.

The roadway dwindled to become a trail that led farther into the wilderness. This was the area McAndrew had proposed to develop. Now Joe knew they couldn't let it happen.

He tried to spot the treasured eagles. Instead, he startled a small flock of wild turkeys who were feeding on acorns. How different the clumsy turkeys were from the graceful eagles.

Yet in their own way both were valuable and important in nature's scheme.

He remembered how in early morning the bald eagles circled the ponderosa pines and swooped down to the lake for food. It was a glorious sight to see the magnificent birds riding the wind, their wingspan so broad that they made shadows on the earth. Oh, how Marla admired them.

Joe struggled over the rough terrain, pausing more than once to catch his breath in the high, thin altitude. He stepped on a dry branch and startled a deer who bounded away. He figured he was about eight thousand feet up now. They should be close.

He shaded his eyes and scanned the treetops. At last he spotted one. An eagle's nest! The complex structure was almost as big as his office. Joe slumped against a boulder and lay back to gaze up at the huge nest made of interlaced branches. Marla would love seeing this.

It was amazing, when you examined the nest. Amazing and beautiful and necessary. So was the eagle. It was a rare bird worth saving.

Worth doing whatever was necessary to save it?

There was only one answer. Yes.

It was the same with his people. They were worth saving, worth helping, worth doing what was necessary to make it possible. And that was his job . . . no, it was his dedication. His commitment. Some things, however unpleasant, had to be done for the good of many. This was one of them. It couldn't be helped.

He would explain it all next week when she came up to the cabin. She would understand. She would hate it, but she would understand.

He hated it, too.

I love you and would never do anything purposely to hurt you. But this is out of my hands. Marla, my love, please understand!

Joe pushed himself to his feet and started back. A wild cry, a high-pitched scream, taunted him. He looked up and saw the eagle's underbelly as it swooped through the treetops. Then the sun reflected on the white crown of the mighty bald eagle as he lifted his cry of defiance. And victory.

A WEEK LATER Marla drove the winding road to the cabin with her usual growing sense of euphoria. Spring in the White Mountains was as glorious as the autumn, although quite opposite. The leaves that had dropped off in various shades of gold returned in multiple hues of green. New life sprouted in the charred acres; the air and earth were moist. The whole place renewed Marla's spirit and refreshed her outlook. She loved it! She wanted to embrace the world in her happiness as she unlocked the cabin.

The familiar musty smell of the closed-up cabin mingled with a stale smoky fragrance left by the forest fire, and she started opening windows immediately. She dropped her suitcase at the foot of the bed and gazed at the multicolored quilt.

Suddenly she was overwhelmed by the desire to make love with Joe on that bed. She could hardly wait to see him!

When he arrived, she hurled herself into his arms, burying her face against his neck. "Joe, Joe!"

He lifted her off the floor and swung her around, kissing her with such fierceness that she muffled a tiny cry against his lips. "Oh, I've missed you, Marla. Now more than ever."

"Me too," she mumbled between kisses and laughter.

Finally he set her down, although he still held her in his arms. "I preferred the period of the media blitz. At least I got to see you more often."

She smiled with contentment. "And I was beginning to like being domestic when there was someone around to appreciate it once in a while."

"I appreciate everything you do. And you. You're beautiful."

"And you're so lucky, getting to stay up here in the mountains. They're so pretty this time of year."

"Did you notice the new growth in the burned areas?"

She nodded. "I'm surprised to see it recovering so soon."

"We've had crews working to clean up the debris to make it easier for Mother Nature to do her thing." He bent to kiss her again, and what was intended to be affectionate and brief lingered and grew passionate. Joe was reminded that she turned him on more than any woman ever had. One kiss led to another . . . and another. Eventually they gravitated to her bedroom, to her quilt-covered bed.

"I want us to make love here, Joe. We haven't officially christened this place."

Joe remembered his unpleasant mission and tried halfheartedly to object. "Marla, we need to talk."

"Later," she whispered with a secretive smile. Unbuttoning his shirt, she began kissing his chest and a line down his taut belly while she fumbled with his belt buckle. Frustrated when the thing wouldn't budge easily, she shoved his hands to his belt. "You get that. I'll take care of me." And she began peeling off her clothes.

"Do you hear me?"

"Talk later," she said. "Do you know how many times I've thought of making love to you up here in this cabin, in this bed? Come on."

"I can't stay long."

"We'll make it quick."

He felt his will weakening as she stripped naked and turned back the quilt. She was beautiful and her urging was too persuasive. He'd tried...he'd tell her later. Right now he couldn't resist.

Her pale, silky body was waiting for him, writhing enticingly on the bed. She wanted him and it was exciting and arousing to have her clutching and caressing, urging with her hands as well as her daring kisses. She fulfilled his every dream in a woman and only a fool would stop right now to talk, especially with what he had to say. So he relinquished his will and allowed his male prowess to take over.

She was luxurious, soft and warm. She met him with anticipation and eagerness, and he found her wildly sexy and exciting. As she explored every part of his body with curious, roving hands, he groaned with the unsurpassed pleasure. Then he returned the bliss, caressing and stroking each curvy, feminine inch of her. Finally, as their bodies combined, sizzling everywhere they touched, he could bear the sweet agony no longer.

She moved sensuously beneath him, guiding him surely into her lush warmth. He rocked with nature's rhythm, hard, fast, hot. And she moved with him. Her soft cry of ecstasy was muffled against his mouth, and he felt her climactic shudder join his.

THE ROOM WAS pitch-black when they awoke. Somehow, sometime, they had curled up in each other's arms and slept. It was truly like heaven.

They showered together. Marla wore a smug smile. Joe was unusually quiet.

"You hungry?" Not bothering with underwear, she pulled her jeans over her slender hips and snapped them. Then she grabbed a sweater and slithered into it.

He watched her pert breasts disappear beneath the soft sweater. "A little."

"You're always hungry," she teased. "How about some canned chili?"

"Okay." He reached for his jeans. "Then we can talk."

She gave him a curious glance. "Sure, Joe." Rather than pursue it now, she headed for the kitchen. *He has something serious on his mind,* she concluded. There were signs, like body language and troubled eyes. And he was unusually quiet. What could be wrong? "Would you make a fire while I heat up the chili?" she asked when he joined her.

"Glad to."

Soon the place was redolent with spicy chili, and the fireplace blazed merrily. Marla brought a tray into the living room bearing the steaming chili in oversize mugs and tortilla chips heaped in a blanket. "Let's eat in here by the fire. It's cozier."

Joe ached inside as they settled before the fire. How could he do this right now? And yet he must.

He didn't know exactly where to start. She took several bites of her chili, so he did, too. "Marla, I need to tell you some of our plans."

"Whose? Ours?"

"The tribe's."

"Oh." She scooped chili onto a chip and popped it into her mouth.

"It's really a good plan, Marla. Josh and I have spent hours on it and so have many tribal leaders. It's getting good response. It's going to be wonderful in many respects, not so great in others."

Marla leaned back against the raised stone hearth. "How? What are you talking about?"

"You know we've been looking for workable solutions to McAndrew's proposal." He was no longer hungry and shoved his bowl aside.

"You came up with something competitive?" She squeezed his hand. "Joe, I'm so proud of you. What is it?"

He stiffened slightly at her display of affection. Guilt was driving him crazy. "We're going to launch a building project ourselves. We'll use Apache workers as much as possible, then contract it out to others. But the whole thing will remain in our control."

"What a great idea!" She beamed at him and noticed his still-strained expression. So what could possibly be wrong with that?

"It won't be condos, though," he continued in a rush. "We're going to recommend a large, resort-type hotel, with the most modern conveniences and glamorous amenities. There'll be several restaurants with Indian, Mexican and Continental cuisines, various shops, including ski shops for rental and purchase. It'll be large enough to accommodate corporate conventions or conferences."

"Very smart," she said with a slow nod. "Good potential for the future."

"Think so?" His heart leaped with hope. Maybe she'd understand, after all.

"Absolutely!"

"But the best part is the Apache Cultural Center and what it will offer my people. Actually, they can make of it what they want. And I'm pleased with the heritage room, which was my Aunt Minnie's idea. She's really excited about all this."

"I'll bet."

"We've already talked to a couple of Indian architects. It'll be designed in harmony with the land."

"Sounds fantastic, Joe."

"The location has been the biggest problem."

"Why? There are so many beautiful places up here."

In a spontaneous and guilt-ridden act he took her hand. "Well, we're not sure yet since we haven't made the presentation to the full council. That won't be done until after the election." Why didn't he just say it?

"I hope you aren't thinking of the high pines area. Remember the eagles."

"No, we certainly wouldn't put it near the eagle nests."

"What area has enough room for a complex of this size and magnitude?"

"We'll have to have good access and room for parking. Good roads and . . ." He felt like hell. "And for a resort like this, it would have to be scenic. That's what attracts the tourist."

She nodded and waited.

"Right now the most logical place appears to be right here, around High Meadow Lake."

There was a moment of dead silence as she digested what he was saying. A dry stick in the fire popped, and somewhere a coyote howled.

"Here? But how? You've got all these houses here."

He sought her eyes as he spoke. "I guess they'd have to be moved."

She paused. "What?"

"I know. It won't be easy." He found himself rushing to explain. "And it's going to be very complicated. But I wanted you to know that this is one of the areas being seriously considered for this project. And it seems to be the best because of its physical assets."

"What would you do with—" She gestured and left her hand midair.

"Well, our lawyer suggests terminating the leases and—"

"What?" Marla's voice was shrill, and she was on her feet now as she realized what he was saying. *This* was what he'd been trying to explain all evening! No wonder he'd been unusually quiet. "What do you mean, terminate our leases? Why, you can't do that!"

"Yes, we can. The land is ours. We'd just be calling it back."

"But we homeowners have contracts!"

"There is a lease-terminating clause."

"But I thought—My dad always thought—"

"I know. Most people thought it would never end, that it was too good for both parties. The Indians thought so, too. But now, Marla, it isn't. Times have changed. We have better things to do with the land." He stood to face her, wanting to take her in his arms, but not daring.

"How can you possibly say that?"

"Because it's true. Can't you understand? This complex is something that will help my people now and for many years to come."

"I don't understand how you could possibly think up something so absolutely crazy!"

"Marla, it's the logical solution."

"Logical? Or heartless?" Tears pooled in her dark eyes as she gaped at him.

When he saw her reaction, he recoiled as if she'd hit him. "Depends on which view you have."

"Or which side of the lake you live on?"

"No," he explained patiently. "If the plan goes through and the leases are terminated, it won't matter if the occupants are Anglo or Indian. They'll all have to move."

She touched her head and felt slightly dizzy. Move? She couldn't believe her ears. Move from this place she loved? This place her dad built? Not without a fight! She narrowed her eyes at him. "I'll sue."

"Won't do much good."

"I have my rights."

"So do we. The land is ours. We've talked to our lawyers at great length. You'll still have your cabin to do with as you see fit—"

"I . . . I can't stand this. Get out." She took a shaky breath, trying to control her wildly raging emotions. "Get out, Joe. I don't see how you could possibly propose something like this. You knew how I felt about the cabin."

"Yes."

"And you still had the nerve—"

"It was out of my hands."

"It was your damned idea!"

"No, it grew from a variety of ideas and people. You knew we were working on something as a counteroffer. Josh and I hacked several ideas around until this one started taking shape. We had other contributors whose opinions I value. Aunt Minnie and her friend Rose, as well as a group of Apache leaders worked on it. This doesn't belong to one. It belongs to many."

"Damn you, Joe Quintero. I set you up and this is how you repay me! I . . . I can't believe it!"

"Marla, I—"

"No! I don't want to hear any more. I can't stand the sight of you right now. You make love to me, then detonate this bombshell!"

"Please try to understand—"

"Don't do that! Just get out! Get out of my sight!" She felt slightly hysterical and could feel sobs welling up inside her,

uncontrollably. She had to get contro...
through. But first she had to get awa...
leave." Her voice quavered. "The way I...
think I ever want to see you again!" She...
bedroom and slammed the door.

Joe didn't stay. There was no use. He...
ing that he couldn't possibly have m...
things, couldn't have told her more rud...
her worse.

He didn't return the next day. Act...
She didn't want to see him. She was to...
full of the upcoming election news...
ponent's were sprinkled among the A...
understand. She walked by the lake,...
Only constant reminders that some...
leave all this.

The next morning she closed th...
Phoenix. It was impossible to relax...
had about the future. She knew that...
her life forever. She wished she'd ne...
vently that she didn't love him.

ON THE APACHE ELECTION DAY Ma...
busy. She worked late at the office...
tion on the way home, hoping to...
herself she didn't care, that Joe Q...
more. But deep inside she knew s...

She was hurt, though. And s...
would do anything to destroy wha...
her. She kept expecting to hear fro...
dropped the idea or had moved t...
spot.

As she turned into her parking spot, a brief news summary came on the air. Before she could flip the dial, she heard that Joseph Quintero had defeated the incumbent, Ben Cartaro. Joe was the new High Meadow Apache chairman.

Marla switched the radio off quickly. So what's the big deal? It wasn't much of a race. Cartaro had served his limit. She knew all along that Joe was the chosen one.

Marla felt sick; her stomach churned. Now Joe could promote whatever future plans he had for the Apache's welfare. He could remove the cabins and build the complex. He could forget her. She placed her hands at the top of the steering wheel and laid her forehead on them. And she sobbed.

JOSH POPPED the champagne cork and poured a little bit of bubbly into every glass extended toward him. He went around the room, laughing and exchanging congratulatory remarks. When he reached his brother, the newly elected Apache leader, he paused. "I notice a particular blond beauty missing from this happy celebration."

"Yep." Joe took a sip of his champagne and set the glass on a table. "Don't expect her, either."

"Oh? Too bad. She's missing a grand celebration and the finest hour for the Quintero family."

"I'm sure she doesn't care to celebrate this occasion."

"Look, bro, I don't mean to pry, but I like the lady. And I know you took a shine to her."

"It's over between us," Joe said tightly.

"Does it have to do with our brilliant concept?"

"That's right. She lives too close to the lake. And she doesn't understand."

"Did you expect her to?"

"Yeah. Is that too unreasonable?"

"Maybe."

Joe turned and walked away, trying to mask his inner sadness with a smile. After all, he'd just won an election. He accepted another congratulatory handshake.

12

MARLA THOUGHT about it for a long time before she decided to send Joe a congratulatory telegram. She just couldn't let his winning the election pass unnoticed, after all they'd been to each other. And as she suspected—feared—he called her upon receiving it. Their conversation was stilted and clumsy, with both of them fumbling around the real issue. Finally she asked if there had been a change of plans.

He said, "No, things are moving forward. We'll be taking our proposal to the council next week. I'll let you know."

"Don't bother."

"Marla, please. Listen to me. Can't we—"

"No, Joe. We can't." She hung up, still gripping the phone with white-knuckled fingers. *Dammit, Joe! How can you do this? How?*

Another two weeks passed until she heard from him. This time it wasn't personal. His message came in a polite but clearly stated form letter. Marla sat at her desk, staring at the sheet. She didn't know whether to cry or scream obscenities. Or both. She made a couple of phone calls, one to her mother. But she received no satisfaction.

"Excuse me, Marla." Letty entered with a steaming cup of coffee and set it on the corner of the desk. She'd been around long enough to know when her boss was upset. "Um, you okay?"

Marla pressed her lips together. She would not cry. But she might vent some steam. "Close the door, please, Letty."

The older woman, who had been a friend as well as a secretary for three and a half years, crossed the room and quietly shut the door. Then she sat in the chair where she usually took dictation or exchanged information about a client. "Can I help with anything, Marla?"

"Probably not," Marla muttered cryptically. "But since you asked, you can listen."

Letty smiled gently. "I'm good at listening."

"Read this." Marla flipped Letty the page, typed on stationery with the impressive High Meadow Apache logo across the top.

Letty read the paper quietly, then let it drop to her lap. "This means your cabin, doesn't it?"

Marla nodded. "My family's cabin, the one my father built. The place I've loved for years, where I've always vacationed—escaped to! How can they do this to us? Why, there are several hundred cabins around that lake!"

"They can't displace everyone, can they?"

"Oh, yes. I wasn't the only one to receive this letter. I've already talked to our neighbors, the Bankses. They received the same letter and have been in touch with the president of our neighborhood association of leaseholders to see if there's something we can do."

"Well, what are your rights?"

"I don't really know. I've read the original contract that Dad signed so many years ago, and it's full of legalese gibberish. The only things I understand are the terms of the lease. That is, the amount we pay and the services they provide. It's pretty straightforward."

"Hasn't the original contract been renegotiated?"

"Not the entire original. Amendments changed the fees with each renewal, which the leaseholders have always agreed to and paid with no hassle." Marla's voice grew harsher. "And now that the Apache have their so-called 'new blood' in as chairman with all his fancy new ideas, they hit us up with this!"

"I have a feeling that's what's bothering you the most, Marla," Letty said gently. "The fact that Joe's the 'new blood,' and that he's behind this whole thing."

"Look, it's my cabin, and I don't want to lose it! It's as simple as that, Letty. Why, I have so many wonderful memories connected with that place that it would be like losing a part of the family. I'd be furious no matter who—"

"But you and I know that without Joe's influence, the Apache probably wouldn't be doing this right now. Joe is their leader, and he's in charge of this project."

"All right. Hell, yes, I'm angry about it!" Marla pushed herself to her feet and paced beside the double windows. "I'm damned angry that Joe would do such a thing . . . to me. And I'm . . . hurt." She rubbed her hand over her face as if to wipe her hurt feelings away. But it didn't work. "I don't know what to do. I feel so helpless."

"Have you talked to Joe?"

"A little. It's useless. He's convinced this is best for his people. He won't even listen to my side anymore."

"Well, it's probably a lousy suggestion, considering your, uh, relationship with Joe, but . . ." Letty paused and looked up at Marla.

"What?" Marla whirled around. Her anger had crowded out logic and love, and right now all she wanted to do was lash out. "There is no relationship, Letty. This has undermined everything. I haven't seen him in weeks. So what were you going to say?"

Letty weighed her thoughts, then proceeded slowly. "The only thing I can think for you to do is to fight, especially if you think you've been wronged, Marla."

"Fight? You mean legal action." She sighed. She hadn't really wanted to fight so hard.

"Talk to a lawyer. How about David Ingram, the one who helps us occasionally? He can certainly explain the original contract and interpret the legalese, as you call it. Maybe you can file a class action suit, one that will include the other cabin owners."

A gleam lit Marla's dark eyes as she felt a renewal of spirit. "Yes, you're absolutely right, Letty. I threatened to sue but didn't follow up on it. Now, why not? They're pushing me to the limit. A class action suit might be the best way to go. Get David on the phone and set up an appointment. Also the president of our neighborhood association. She's in the book under, uh . . ."

"I know." Letty headed for the door. "High Meadow Lake."

Marla rubbed her hands together. "This will show them they can't push us around. Won't Joe be surprised when the whole tribe is hit with a lawsuit from every cabin owner!"

TWO DAYS LATER Marla sat across from David Ingram's desk, her arms folded, her mouth set. "So what's the angle, David. Do we have the grounds to sue?"

David leafed through the file of papers Marla had delivered previously for his analysis. "In a word, Marla, no."

"What?" She sat upright, her brown eyes snapping. "Then I'll get someone else! Someone with enough guts to go against the Indians."

"Go ahead, but you'll run into the same problem. Unless someone takes you for a legal ride."

She sighed and slumped back in the chair. A weak smile of apology crossed her face. "Sorry, David. I didn't mean to doubt you. I guess I had my hopes up too much."

"I warned you on the phone, Marla."

"I know, but I'm just so . . ."

"Disturbed." He smiled sympathetically. "But it's understandable."

"I was going to say desperate." Actually, she felt distraught as David crushed her hopes.

"Look, Marla. I would love the challenge of a case like this, if I felt there were sufficient grounds for winning. But there aren't. I'd only make a fool of myself and cost you a lot of money. The facts are that the Indians own the land. And they want it back. In the letter they're giving you the option of taking what you own, which is the cabin. If you refuse that option, the cabin becomes theirs when your lease expires in one year. And they can do with it what they wish. Use it or tear it down."

"That's not fair!"

"But they're giving you fair warning. They're giving you the option. They're saying, in effect, 'please take your cabin. We don't want it.'"

Marla swallowed hard. "You're sure, David?"

The young lawyer adjusted his wire-rimmed glasses. "I'm sure, Marla. Plain and clear."

"Only if you understand legal doublespeak," she mumbled, feeling herself sink into a bottomless abyss. "So I'm caught?"

"Not entirely. If I were you, Marla, I'd move the cabin to another property. And make sure you own it outright this time."

"Move it?" She sighed and considered the thought seriously for the first time. "Move it. Yes, that's what I'll do. I'll have the cabin moved." She stood and shook hands with renewed determination. "Thanks, David. I'll move it."

A WEEK LATER Marla donned a yellow hard hat and hiked over clods of dry, freshly grated earth. "Mr. Baumbauer, I got your message, but I wanted to speak to you in person about this."

The heavyset man wearing a matching yellow hard hat and dirt-streaked khaki shirt stared at her. "What're you doing out here, lady?"

"I'm Marla Eden," she amended, thinking this was no way to conduct business. But when one was desperate, one didn't think about protocol. "We talked on the phone several times. I'm the one who called to see if you could move my cabin from High Meadow."

"Oh, yes." He grinned. "Nice cabin, Ms Eden. Real sturdy."

"Did you actually go up there and inspect everything, Mr. Baumbauer—"

"Look, nobody calls me mister. You call me Rudy."

"Rudy, then." She looked at him impatiently. "I'm very distressed that you think it's too much of a risk."

"My foreman and I inspected that place personally. It's solid as a mountain."

"Apparently you don't understand, Rudy. I must have that cabin moved. *Must.*" She felt as though she were hyperventilating, but maybe it was just the wind on the construction site. "I have to have it moved. If I don't, the Indians are going to destroy it."

"Real sorry. Can't."

"What do you mean, can't? It's impossible?"

"Naw, it ain't that. Nothing's impossible. But it's gonna cost you a pretty penny. Other problem is, I can't guarantee the whole damned thing wouldn't fall apart if I tried to take it. My insurance won't cover such a risk. If it was mine, I wouldn't take the chance."

"But you're moving the Bankses' cabin. They recommended you." Marla's voice was a whine picked up by the wind and whisked away.

"Theirs is made different. Here, let me show you," Rudy said, putting a pencil to the page on his clipboard. He started to draw, and Marla could tell right away it was a crude sketch of her cabin. "Here's the problem. That damned thing—uh, excuse me, ma'am—that cabin is made so well that if we tried to move it, why it might just crack right down the middle. Here—" he drew arrows "—or here. It's constructed of a variety of materials, mostly logs and rocks, which won't hang together when we start messing around with 'em. Now you could move it log by log, but that's gonna cost you what two cabins are worth."

"I . . . I can't afford that."

"Most of us can't. Anyway, that fireplace is built to last forever. It has to stay where it's planted."

Marla gazed bleakly at the sketches. She blinked back tears. Rudy's company had been recommended as one of the best movers. His was the third to tell her the same thing. She had to believe them, had to accept their evaluations. But it hurt. "So the fireplace is there forever, unless someone comes along and tears it down."

"Yep." Rudy nodded matter-of-factly.

"Dammit, Rudy!"

He gave her a quick look of surprise. "Yes, ma'am. Sorry about that. I was hoping we could do business. Now if you have anything else that needs—" He halted when Marla wheeled around. Shoving his hard hat back with his thumb, he watched her hike out of the construction site.

Marla swatted blindly at her tears. *Now what?* She knew. When one was desperate, it called for desperate action.

MARLA JERKED her blue Honda to a stop beside the shiny red Jeep in the parking lot. There was no other alternative, no one else to turn to. She had tried working within the system. When all her attempts failed, she felt defeated. Now she was willing to do anything. She would try one final appeal. Swallowing her pride, she stomped up the steps to the High Meadow Apache Tribal Building.

"I'm Marla Eden," she said to the woman at the front desk. "I have an appointment with J—, er, with Mr. Quintero."

"Right this way."

Marla followed the dark-haired woman and squared her shoulders just before entering the office at the end of the hallway. She thought she was prepared for seeing Joe again, but the sight of him was like an assault, a whirlwind that took her breath. She stared at him for a moment, gathering her resources, reaching deep inside for her anger. She thought she'd discarded her emotional attachment to him long ago, but it clouded her vision again.

"Joe . . ."

"Marla . . ."

Joe stood up behind the large desk when she entered the room. He looked devastating in a white dress shirt with the collar open and the sleeves casually rolled up to his elbows. His copper skin and dark hair matched those around him now. He seemed to belong in this office filled with artifacts and remnants of his Indian ancestry. A large Apache burden basket hung in the corner, a group of coiled baskets decorated one wall near a prayer stick with eagle feathers. Reminders of his past and of the future.

Yet there was something different in his sharp, ebony eyes that caught her attention. Something poignant and grave. And as her eyes inadvertently traveled over him, she thought he seemed a little slimmer than when they were in Mexico where she'd seen—and felt—his bare body on almost a daily basis. The memory sent a flush through her.

He licked his lips and spoke in a hushed voice. "Please have a seat. It's good to see you. You look . . . beautiful, as always, Marla."

She ignored his attempt at dredging up old feelings and strode into the room, assuming an air of indifference. But it was all part of an act because she certainly didn't feel it. She wanted to ask if he'd lost weight, but instead said, "You seem to have taken your job as chairman seriously. Already moving and shaking, I see."

"I take my position very seriously, Marla. I thought you understood that all along."

"If I didn't realize your dedication before, you've made it perfectly clear now."

"Right." He pursed his lips and nodded. "Would you like coffee or a Coke?"

"No, thank you. I'm here on business. Nothing more."

"I see." He dropped back down into his chair and kept his gaze steadily on her. "How . . . how are you?"

Her face tightened. "As if you care."

"I do."

"Do you really care what happens to me?"

"Of course!" He leaned forward urgently, his forearms resting on the desk. "Marla, some things haven't changed. Feelings—"

"Then prove it by helping me." She gripped her purse as the words tumbled out. "Help me save my cabin, Joe. You're the only one I can turn to. And you're in a position to do something."

"Marla, the council voted—"

"I've heard that before," she said, interrupting with a wave of her hand. Leaning forward, she continued her barrage of words. "You *can* do something if you will. You are my last resort, Joe. I've been to my lawyer. Yes, I considered suing," she said bitterly when he looked surprised. "Oh, God, how I wanted to. It would have given me great pleasure to see you back down." She thought it would give her pleasure to see him squirm. But there was no pleasure in this. He wasn't squirming. She was begging.

"Are you going to sue?"

"Unfortunately, no. My lawyer says you're covered in the original contract. So that idea went down the tubes."

"Too bad your pleasure was foiled," Joe muttered, leaning back in his chair.

"Next I talked to three different contractors about moving the cabin, like you suggested in your damned eviction letter. Some of my neighbors are already making such plans."

"Unfortunately it's the only way."

"I even picked out a lot near Show Low and was on the verge of buying it," she recounted with a mocking chuckle. "But they can't move my cabin because of the way it's constructed. Too sturdy, wouldn't you know? I could do more harm than good trying to move it. The best they could do would be to dismantle the whole thing and reconstruct it on another lot for a fee well above its actual worth." She paused for a breath. "But that's far beyond my funding ability. Piles of rocks and logs would probably lie on the lot for years before I could make them into a cabin again. So I'm asking for your help."

"Would you like to borrow money, Marla? I'll be glad—"

"No, I don't want your money! I want you to change the plans. Set your project somewhere else. Do something to preserve the lake residences."

He spread his hands. "Marla, I can't."

"You mean you won't."

"No. I can't. The project has been drawn up into a formal proposal, complete with goals and functions, a schedule of constructing each stage and projections for the future. It's out of my hands. Other people are working on it. We have a project director. The architect is working on a mock-up now. The first drawings are complete."

"My house will be destroyed, Joe." She paused and choked down a sob. "Don't you care about that?"

"Yes, of course."

"You helped fight the fire to save it last year! And now you're going to stand by and let it be demolished?"

"I had no idea it would come to this. I thought you would be able to move it."

"How could you let this happen so fast? Why, you weren't in office a month when your secretary efficiently sent out the eviction notices."

"Those letters weren't eviction notices. They were carefully worded so as to ease this process as much as possible."

"How considerate of you. At any rate, you've lost no time in getting right to work on this. The sooner the better, I suppose."

"I did not try to rush this, Marla. Things were happening with McAndrew. We had to do something. Now was just the time."

"I don't know why I thought you would help me, Joe."

"Marla, you're thinking of one person. Yourself. I have to think of a whole community of people. I'm concerned with their welfare, with their future. That's what this is all about."

"Obviously you don't give a damn about my future. Or ours."

"Yes, I do. I hoped you'd listen. Because you've lived up here, I thought you'd understand. I want to work this out."

"Understand? I'm losing something intensely important to me, a part of my past—my life—that will never be the same again, and you act as if I should be gracious and generous. Sorry, Joe." She stood and walked steadily to the door.

"So am I, Marla." He watched her go, feeling like the biggest heel in the world with the heavy weight of leadership square on his shoulders and a great sadness in his heart.

Even after all this time and the bitter words exchanged between them, he knew that what he felt for this woman was love. Love beyond reason and understanding. And he was losing that love because of something he'd originated and directed. And he could do nothing to stop either.

13

IT HAD BEEN a scorcher all week with temperatures over 110 degrees for five straight days. The radio stations led their newscast with the local weather. Marla was tired of the heat and tired of hearing about it. She switched off the radio and shoved a cassette into the tape deck, thinking she should be in the White Mountains right now. This was when she usually took a break from Phoenix's incessant heat and escaped to the cabin. Her time there was limited, so why was she staying away?

She knew. She was afraid of running into Joe.

Dammit, he was responsible for her losing the cabin. But she shouldn't let him keep her from enjoying her last year there. She'd check her calendar and plan a mountain trip sometime soon. Maybe next week. Satisfied with her decision, she began humming with the tape. Abruptly she halted. The song was Air Supply's beautiful rendition of "Now and Forever." She recalled listening to it with Joe . . . and how they'd talked and drawn closer and made love. . . .

No! She couldn't do this to herself! Everything brought memories of Joe. And yes, she had been fool enough to think their relationship, their love, would last forever. And it just hadn't.

The knock on her door was so low that she could hardly hear it over the music. She wasn't expecting anyone and wasn't dressed for company, but the knocking continued, so she went to the door and looked through the peephole.

Joe! As if some witchcraft made him appear when she least wanted to see him.

Marla jerked the door open, suddenly filled with fire. He stood there boldly, wearing a white shirt and khaki pants, looking as devastating as she'd ever seen him. A rush of heat surrounded him and pushed inside her air-conditioned room. She braced herself and muttered, "You've got nerve, coming here after our last encounter!"

"I know. Can I come in so we can talk?"

"About what? I have nothing more to stay to you."

"Well, I have something to say to you. It's about the cabin."

Marla hesitated. She figured he'd come around to try to mend the rift that had torn them apart. She hadn't expected him to have any other interest, like the cabin. "You said it was out of your hands."

"It is. But I have . . . Marla, can I come in?"

She uttered a resigned sigh and stepped back.

Joe entered the coolness of her apartment. The familiar music surrounded him, filling him with memories and old feelings. She was dressed in pale blue shorts and a matching pullover. Her blond hair was twisted up on her head, and a few tendrils escaped seductively around her face. She looked fabulous, and he was overwhelmed with the desire to take her in his arms and soothe her hurt feelings. And repair the damaged relationship that kept them apart. But he could do neither.

He gazed at her with incredible sadness in his deep ebony eyes. A tightness gripped his chest as a rush of old feelings surfaced, and he wanted to reach out, to touch her, to hold her close. But he didn't dare. His hands flexed in frustration.

"I thought you might come up to the mountains to get out of this heat," he began weakly.

So he *had* been watching for her. "I couldn't get away."

"Working hard, Marla?"

She nodded. *What else is there to do? Sit around and think about lost loves?* "And you, Joe?"

He shook his head wearily. "Every day another challenge. One headache after another. But we're making small accomplishments that balance it out." *I wish you were there to share them with me.*

"Is the job everything you expected?" *Or do you wish you'd never agreed to it?*

"I'm doing exactly what I want to do. I'm needed there and that's important." *I need you there with me, Marla.*

"Yes, I suppose it is." She gestured toward a chair, "Have a seat since you're here. I'm sure you didn't stop by to talk about the weather or our jobs."

"Right." He moved across the room and settled into a barrel chair. His chest strained his shirt, and his long arms curved around the chair, making his shoulders appear even broader. When he crossed his ankle over his knee, he looked powerfully masculine. One large brown hand rested on his ankle, and she noticed he wore a massive turquoise ring now. He was incredibly handsome, and Marla struggled with her self-control. Lord, how she still loved the man!

For a crazed moment she wondered what difference anything else made. Their love was all that mattered.

She took a deep breath, regaining control of her emotions, and sat in the chair opposite him.

"Marla, I . . ." He halted and looked at her.

"Yes?" She lifted her dark eyes to meet his. "Would you like something to drink? I have Perrier or sparkling water."

"No, thanks. I . . . You know, you look fabulous, Marla. I miss you."

She squeezed her hands together. "I'm sure as you get busy, you'll forget all about me."

"No, Marla. I'll never forget you. I'll never lose this feeling for you."

"Joe—"

"No, that's not why I came here tonight. But when I saw you again, in this place, our music, everything the same yet so awfully different . . . I don't know, Marla. Something just came over me, and I had to say. . . I still feel the same way about you." He looked away and sighed. "I hadn't intended on making that speech at all. But now that it's out, at least you know where I stand."

Do I? she thought, pushing herself to her feet. "I can't listen to this, Joe. I just can't."

"Look, I'm sorry. Forget it."

She walked away from where he was seated. "I wish I could. Wish I could forget everything."

There was silence, then Joe said, "Marla, do you know what we're saying here?"

"Don't interpret anything, Joe. We have problems, big ones. Some that I can't overlook, even if you can. Or think you can. We come from different worlds. We took a chance and it didn't work out. That's all there is to it. I'm glad we both found out before it was too late."

"You don't want to try to patch things up?"

"Is that what you came here for?"

"No."

"Then what?"

"I came to give you some of your own advice. And to make a suggestion—that you can certainly refuse if you want— about the cabin."

She turned around slowly and curiously approached him again. "My own advice?"

He placed both feet on the floor, then leaned forward in the chair. "You see, I'm an attentive student, Marla. I've applied many of the things you taught me to a wide variety of circumstances. For instance, remember the negotiating techniques you helped me memorize before I faced McAndrew in Mexico? There's yes, no, give me more information, give me more time and the counteroffer. Now, you're telling me that you can't take the option offered by the tribe to move your cabin."

"Moving might tear it apart. And dismantling and reconstructing would cost thousands. So . . ."

"So your answer is no."

She nodded. "Not my choice, but it's what I'm stuck with."

"Well, why not make a counteroffer?"

"A counter? I thought that's what we discussed in your office."

"Not to me. I told you, it's out of *my* hands. Make it to the High Meadow Apache Tribe."

"Like what?" She gave him a derisive chuckle. "'On bended knees I'm begging you to scrap this project!'"

"That isn't a counteroffer. That's begging."

"It's all I have left!" She felt near tears.

"That's not so, Marla." His tone was low and calm. "I have an idea."

His tone attracted her, and she sat down again. "What?"

"I think it's understood that you can't keep the cabin and live in it the way you have in the past years."

"Yes, you've made that perfectly clear."

"And you won't move the cabin for fear of tearing it apart, right?"

"Absolutely. Otherwise, I'd have it moved immediately."

"So your goal now should be to keep your father's cabin from being destroyed."

"That seems impossible. If I don't move it, the Indians will tear it down after it's abandoned."

"Not if you propose a good use for the cabin. A counter-offer."

She frowned. "What are you talking about, Joe?"

He leaned farther forward, bracing his elbows on wide-spread knees. "Think about this. What if you offered something in exchange for occasional use of the cabin?"

"Something? Like money? I thought we'd been through that and the Indians want the land, not more rent."

"That's right. We do. And money—" he shrugged "—that's not the issue here. We figure to make more money in the long run by getting rid of the cabins."

"So what could I offer?"

"A service. Something we don't have, something we need or could use."

"A service? From me?"

"Exactly. Something you, and only you, can offer. Like classes in Smile, Rise and Shine. Or the Speak Easy techniques. Teach our people some of your skills. Organize a short program that you could give several times a year in exchange for a few weeks' vacation in the cabin."

She considered this suggestion for a moment. "Well, I've often thought I'd like to develop a program that could be used in high schools. If we could teach young people to be at ease and to communicate better at earlier ages, we wouldn't have adults who are terrified of standing in front of a crowd to speak."

"Then why don't you develop a pilot program for teens? And present it to the council. I think it's a great idea, Marla."

"And how would the cabin fit into this?"

"You'd have to show how it could be used year-round."

"It wouldn't be . . . just mine?"

"No, I'm afraid that situation will have to stand. But if we can—er, you can show how the building itself can be put to good use, perhaps we can persuade the committee not to tear it down." His broad hands gestured, almost imploring her to agree. "Marla, I don't think it's possible now for you to keep the cabin for yourself. Not at this point, with the structural problems in moving it. What I'm suggesting may possibly save the cabin from destruction, though."

"But I would be able to stay in it?"

He nodded enthusiastically. "Maybe it could be slated for VIP use. For you or others who come to the reservation, like dignitaries who might attend special events."

She gave him a tiny smile. "For the newly elected chairman to live in?"

"No. I'm building my own place. I don't need it. Another thought is that it could be used by people, maybe kids, who live on remote parts of the reservation and come to the Cultural Center for classes or special events. Its use could be monitored by a committee to make sure it's kept in good shape. And it could continue to be a special place." Joe clasped his hands between his knees and gazed at her expectantly.

She sighed and rubbed her forehead with two fingers. "I don't know what to say."

"Say yes."

She bit her lip and leaned back. "I need . . ."

"I know, I know. You need time to think about it." He stood up and stuffed his hands into his hip pockets.

"Exactly."

"I understand. Well, think about it, Marla. I suggest that you work up a plan and present it yourself at the next council meeting. This whole proposal will be more effective if it comes from you."

"You're probably right." She stood up to face him. "I'll...I'll let you know."

"The meeting is in two weeks, on Thursday night." He dropped his hands to his sides and took a few steps toward the door. "I'll support you any way I can. You can rely on my yes vote."

"Joe?"

He stopped and turned around.

"Thanks."

He nodded silently and started toward the door again.

"Joe . . ." She waited until he faced her again. "Would you . . . like to stay . . . for dinner?"

He chuckled. "I can't believe I'm saying this, but no, thanks. I have an appointment with a local TV station. They're going to tape an interview about the project. It should air this weekend on one of those noon talk shows."

"Afterward?" She twisted her fingers together.

He gazed at her for a moment and knew he could take her in his arms right now. She'd come willingly. He could see the desire in her eyes. But now was not the time. And this was not the way. He wanted it real, wanted their differences aired and settled, wanted her love, not just their lust. "No, Marla. Not this time. We need to think about it."

"Maybe you do."

"I wouldn't want any regrets tomorrow. Two volunteers, remember?"

She nodded. "Okay. I'll let you know about the counter-offer."

"Call as soon as you've decided. We'll need to put you on the agenda."

"You sound as though you're organized."

He pressed his lips together. "Yep. Well organized and goal oriented. I had a good instructor."

She smiled and he slipped out the door. Without a kiss. Without another word. She watched through the window as his shiny red Jeep drove away. Unbidden tears filled her eyes and overflowed down her cheeks.

IN TWO DAYS Marla and her secretary, Letty, had developed a roughly outlined idea for several one-day self-esteem workshops and two week-long communications workshops for teenagers. They were innovative and unusual, filled with fun activities that were geared to interest teens yet designed to instruct. She was proud of what they'd developed so far. By the end of the week Marla had decided to do it, to give it a whirl.

"Letty, would you call the tribal council and tell them to put me on the agenda?"

"So you're going to go for it?" Letty beamed at her boss. "Atta girl!"

Marla nodded. "I don't know, Letty. Sometimes I think it's futile."

"Go for it, Marla!" Letty gave the air a punch. "Nothing ventured, nothing gained."

"Sounds like grandmotherly advice." Marla smiled at the familiar cliché. "I figured I'd coincide the presentation with a few days in the cabin."

"A little vacation in the mountains," Letty agreed. "That's what you need."

"I hardly think this will be a vacation. I've never been under tighter stress. This is one presentation I have to ace." She whirled her chair around so she could look out the window and nervously hugged her arms.

Not much pressure, Marla thought miserably as she listened to Letty's call to the High Meadow tribal office. This is the most important presentation of my career. Everyone will be listening and observing. Joe will be there. And everything hangs in the balance.

MARLA STOOD in the hallway outside the council room. She didn't know when she'd been so nervous. She smoothed the skirt of her carefully chosen dress, a khaki shirtwaist with a wide belt and unpressed pleats. She hadn't wanted to over-dress, nor to appear too casual. Her rule of thumb to clients was to dress like their clientele or those they were address-ing. She'd carefully reviewed her own rules and applied them to herself and to her particular situation. She tried to make herself calm. But the herd of buffalo in her stomach wouldn't settle down.

As she waited, Marla mentally ran down her list of tips for good presentations. Act relaxed and confident, even when you aren't. Be concise and specific. Deal with hostile re-marks in complete composure. Inhale for five seconds, then exhale slowly. She practiced her breathing.

The door opened and a dark-haired woman motioned. "Ms Eden? You can come on in."

Marla breathed again and plastered a confident smile on her face. She clutched her manila folder and reached for her visual aid, a large cardboard poster on which she'd drawn and labeled blocks to demonstrate her presentation, espe-cially the details of what she'd be teaching.

The circle of dark-haired men gazed solemnly at her when she entered the room. She spotted Joe at the far side and he winked and gave her a thumbs-up sign. Marla propped her visual aid on the requested tripod, but as she turned around to begin her presentation, the poster fell, floating in dra-matic slow motion to the floor.

She told herself to be calm, that this was no tragedy, nor was it an omen. It took her another nervous minute to stoop and retrieve the thing and reprop it. She paused, holding her breath, to see if it would stay. It stayed.

Exhaling in relief, she smiled at the group. She was too nervous to realize she'd already captured their attention with her striking blond-haired beauty. And she had their empathy when her poster fell. They were with her before she even opened her mouth.

"Gentlemen, thank you for having me here tonight and for being willing to listen to me. I know you all have special feelings toward your ancestors. Well, I have ancestors, of course. And my feelings toward them are very special, too. So maybe you can understand when I tell you how I feel about the cabin my father built...."

She had touched a nerve. They listened to every word.

When she was finished, Marla gathered her information and stumbled from the room. She was flushed and excited and had suddenly forgotten everything she ever knew about remaining calm.

Joe followed her. "Why don't you wait in my office, Marla? The council needs to discuss this proposal and take a vote."

She looked at him, a question in her intense eyes.

"You did fine." He nodded, then looked at the woman who'd escorted Marla in and out of the room. "Rona, would you please get Ms Eden some coffee? And she can wait in my office."

"Yes, sir." She smiled at Marla. "Come with me, please."

As if in a daze, Marla followed. In another few minutes she stood in the middle of Joe's office, her paraphernalia piled on his desk, a Styrofoam cup of coffee in her hand. She sipped. The coffee was almost cold. But she didn't care. She drank it, anyway.

"Anything else I can get you, Ms Eden?" Rona stood by the door.

Marla smiled wearily. "If you could influence their vote, that would be appreciated."

"I wish I could," Rona admitted with an encouraging smile. "I just want you to know that I think your program sounds wonderful, especially the part about building self-esteem. I have two teenagers, and I would want my children to take your class."

"Why, thank you, Rona." Marla sighed a little in relief. "I . . . I know it's something the elders have probably never considered, but I feel it's extremely important these days. Especially for the young."

"As a mother, I think it's very important, too. I hope they accept your plan, Ms Eden. I think it would be good for all of us."

"Thank you."

Rona closed the door quietly and left Marla alone. She paced the room, then sat down, crossing and recrossing her legs, trying to stay put. But soon she was pacing again. Thirty minutes seemed like forever. She downed the coffee, then decided she had to go to the bathroom. She waited. What if she were in there when Rona returned? Finally she could wait no longer and used the facility adjoining Joe's office.

She hurriedly returned to the empty office. Still nothing. She checked her watch. It had been an hour. Dammit, what was taking so long!

Then the door opened, and Joe stood on the threshold.

14

"WHAT TOOK SO LONG?"

"Some discussion."

"Wh-what did they say?" Marla looked at him, searched his face for an expression that would tell her something.

His swarthy countenance was impassive. Joe closed the door and walked slowly into his office. "They said, 'How many rooms does this cabin have?' I said, 'It has a large living-dining room combination, a kitchen, a bath and two bedrooms. We can add bunk beds if we need to sleep more.'"

She took a shaky breath. "And . . ."

"I told them the fireplace was hand built from native rocks and so sturdy it might last forever."

She swallowed hard. "Joe—"

He walked slowly toward her. "They said, 'What is this self-esteem she wants to teach our children?' I said, 'She will teach our children to be proud Apache and to lift their heads high. And how to speak in public with confidence.'"

Marla nodded, feeling somewhat frantic. "Yes . . ."

"And they said, 'How does she know about the Apache and what will make them proud?' I said, 'She knows about people.'"

"Oh, Joe . . ." She wrung her hands.

He stopped a few inches from her. "They said, 'Can she teach us to make a speech so that everyone will listen as we listened to her?' And I said, 'Yes, each and every one of you. She knows her stuff.'"

"Joe, you're driving me crazy! What did they say about saving the cabin?"

He paused and smiled slightly. "They said yes."

"Oh, Joe! Thank you!" She bubbled with joy and in her exuberance threw her arms around Joe's shoulders and hugged him with all her might.

Joe's strong arms curled around her back and held her to him, relishing the sensuous pressure of her body against his for the first time in weeks. He held her tightly, even after she'd begun to let go.

When Marla realized that she'd flung herself into his arms, her body went rigid and her hands rested on his shoulders. "Joe..."

"Marla, don't let go. I can't..."

She turned her face up, and his ebony eyes drank in the sight of her alluring blond hair, brown eyes gleaming with tears, creamy-smooth cheeks, slightly smiling strawberry lips. Impulsively he kissed her, long and hard.

His lips molded to hers, forcing them to part, revealing his pent-up passion and the frustration he'd felt during the past few weeks. Joe forgot that he was in his office and the council members were milling around after adjournment and could pop in at any minute. He forgot everything but Marla in his arms, Marla's lips pressed to his, Marla responding.

Something happened to Marla when Joe kissed her. Something quite beyond her control. In the tense moments before they kissed, she had no intention of ending up in his arms. But her joy at saving the cabin coupled with an indistinct knowledge that Joe had been responsible for making that happen erupted into a giddiness, a seeking of the man whom she loved, whom she knew still cared for her.

When he kissed her, she melted inside, melted against him, sought the security of his strong body, held on to the strength of his shoulders. Her fingers dug into his shoulders as she opened her mouth to receive the sweet probing of his tongue.

With no thought to control, she writhed against him, pressing her breasts to his chest. He moved his hands down her back, adjusted her hips to meld with his, spread his fingers wide over the curve of her buttocks, then slid them to her back again. He couldn't touch her enough.

Vaguely they heard the door open behind them.

Joe tore his lips from Marla's and turned his head, still embracing her.

"Excuse me, sir," an embarrassed Rona mumbled, and started to close the door again.

Joe smiled and continued to hold Marla. "That's okay, Rona."

"I, er, just wanted to say good-night, sir. Everyone's gone and, uh, would you lock up?"

"Be glad to." Joe smiled down at Marla. "We should be going, too."

Rona quietly closed his office door.

"Right." Marla tried to push away from Joe, but he kept his arm around her shoulder. "This is no place for such a display of emotions."

"Where is such a place?"

"We could go to my, er, *the* cabin. I understand it's reserved for VIPs. Like the chairman of the Apache."

"I'd like to bypass this emotional display and get right to the passionate part."

"Joe!" She laughed and tried to pull away.

But he held her for another minute. "I love you, Marla. Love you more than anything or anyone could. More than reason. I can't stand to be apart from you any longer. Can't stand to let you go. You know I wanted all along to help you avoid this problem with the cabin. Please believe that."

"I know," she admitted softly. "I was just so hurt for a while that I was blind. But I realize how you were caught and how much you did for me to make tonight possible." She smiled up at him, tears of genuine happiness shining in her eyes. "I love you, too, Joe. And I don't want to lose you. Ever."

"I'd say we were communicating pretty well for a change. And according to my instructor, that's important. Now I'd like to show you my love." He kissed her again.

"I'd like that, too, Joe. Would you like to share my bed in the VIP suite? I believe it's one of the best on the reservation."

"The very best!" He smiled and caressed her hair lovingly. "I've got to hand it to you, honey. You were wonderful before the council. You really know how to practice what you preach."

"I was so nervous."

"You looked cool, and that's what counts."

"Now I know how much easier it is to tell someone how to make an impressive presentation than it is to do it. Especially when so much is at stake."

"You were great."

"I felt your support, Joe."

"Could you also feel the vibes of my love across the room?"

"Yes." She returned his kiss, then whispered her avowal of love.

Then they gathered her paraphernalia and left the Tribal Building arm in arm. Their night together, the first in so long, was glorious. They embraced in a rapid heat of feverish hands, touching and caressing, and murmured words of love.

"Never leave me, Marla. I couldn't stand it again."

"Do you know what you're saying, Joe?"

"That I love you. And I want you with me, always."

"There might be problems with that."

"We'll work them out. Together."

"I love you so much."

They clung together throughout the night, their passion fulfilling unsatisfied longings, their love gentle and healing. And they both knew this was right, the way it should be.

THE EARLY-MORNING SOLITUDE was pierced by the wild cry of the great bald eagle as it swung down from the high pines and swooped over the lake on wide wings. The silvery surface of the lake reflected the rising sun and a single boat with a single fisherman.

"That's Uncle Will," Joe said quietly. "I want you to meet him and Aunt Minnie, Marla. Today."

"I'm ready. But do you think they're ready for me?"

Joe tightened his hold on her hand, intertwining their fingers as they walked along the trail that circled the lake. "They'll love you, Marla. Just as I do."

"I mean, are they ready for us to talk of marriage?"

"Like any other family, they'll want to know if our love is real. Do you really and truly love me? And are my feelings the same toward you?"

"Will there be a problem with me living here?"

"As my wife, you'll be accepted. But you'd be accepted anyway as one who has demonstrated respect for our people and our culture. As a non-Indian, you may be restricted from attending private ceremonies, but I don't think that will affect us. The biggest problem we'll face is getting you to an airport when you need to fly out for business."

"Maybe we can make some arrangements through Show Low's airport."

"And we'll fix a branch office for you in the new house."

She gave a little skip of excitement. "Where will it be built?"

He pointed to a hill overlooking the lake. "Up there. We'll drive to it later in the Jeep. It's rugged land but beautiful. I'm clearing the site as little as possible and having the house built in the middle of the trees. I want to keep it as natural as I can. You'll love it, Marla."

"I'm sure I will. Almost as much as I love you, Joe."

"The place will be ours, Marla. Forever. We'll design it and build it. We'll haul the rocks for the fireplace. We'll make it ours. And maybe it'll help replace your father's cabin in your heart." His voice was low and sincere, and she knew he still regretted her losing the cabin.

"You know, Joe, I'm happy with the future plans for the cabin. Of course, I'm thrilled that it won't be destroyed. But I think its use for boarding kids and visiting dignitaries is something my father would be proud of. In a way, it continues what he endorsed years ago, and that is a sharing and blending of all people."

Joe turned to her and pulled her into his arms. "Do you think your father would approve of us?"

"Absolutely. We've taken that philosophy to the ultimate. To love beyond any limits." She slid her hands around his back and pressed her slender rib cage to his. Suddenly she was filled with an unrestrained euphoria, and she wanted to shout the story of her love to the wind so that it would be carried to all corners of the land.

"Marla, I love you . . . so much."

Their lips melded, their bodies embraced. Joe had captured her completely, body and soul. And Marla had become his willing captive, his love.

As they stood beside the lake, bound together by invisible but everlasting bonds of love, the great bald eagle circled the lake and headed back to the safety of his high country nest. Wings flapping, he rose until he reached a wind current, then sailed effortlessly ever higher. He lifted his triumphant cry to the lofty peaks, home of the mountain spirits and of the wind.

To Marla and Joe it was a proclamation of their everlasting love.

Lynda Ward's TOUCH THE STARS

...the final book in the The Welles Family Trilogy

Lynda Ward's TOUCH THE STARS... the final book in the Welles Family Trilogy. All her life Kate Welles Brock has sought to win the approval of her wealthy and powerful father, even going as far as to marry Burton Welles's handpicked successor to the Corminco Corporation.

Now, with her marriage in tatters behind her, Kate is getting the first taste of what it feels like to really live. Her glorious romance with the elusive Paul Florian is opening up a whole new world to her.... Kate is as determined to win the love of her man as she is to prove to her father that she is the logical choice to succeed him as head of Corminco....

Don't miss TOUCH THE STARS, a Harlequin Superromance coming to you in September.

If you missed the first two books of this exciting trilogy, #317 RACE THE SUN and #321 LEAP THE MOON, and would like to order them, send your name, address and zip or postal code, along with a check or money order for $2.95 for each book ordered (plus $1.00 postage and handling) payable to Harlequin Reader Service to:

In the U.S.	In Canada
901 Fuhrmann Blvd.	P.O. Box 609
Box 1396	Ft. Erie, Ontario
Buffalo, NY 14240-9954	L2A 5X3

LYNDA-1C

Temptation™

TEMPTATION WILL BE
EVEN HARDER TO RESIST...

In September, Temptation is presenting a sophisticated new face to the world. A fresh look that truly brings Harlequin's most intimate romances into focus.

What's more, all-time favorite authors Barbara Delinsky, Rita Clay Estrada, Jayne Ann Krentz and Vicki Lewis Thompson will join forces to help us celebrate. The result? A very special quartet of Temptations...

- **Four striking covers**
- **Four stellar authors**
- **Four sensual love stories**
- **Four variations on one spellbinding theme**

All in one great month! Give in to Temptation in September.

HARLEQUIN SIGNATURE EDITION

VIOLET WINSPEAR

HOUSE OF STORMS

Editorial secretary Debra Hartway travels to the Salvador family's rugged Cornish island home to work on Jack Salvador's latest book. Disturbing questions hang in the troubled air over Lovelis Island. What or who had caused the tragic death of Jack's young wife? Why did Jack stay away from the home and, more especially, the baby son he loved so well? And—why should Rodare, Jack's brother, who had proved himself a man of the highest integrity, constantly invade Debra's thoughts with such passionate, dark desires...?

Violet Winspear, who has written more than 65 romance novels translated worldwide into 18 languages, is one of Harlequin's best-loved and bestselling authors. HOUSE OF STORMS, her second title in the Harlequin Signature Edition program, is a full-length novel rich in romantic tradition and intriguingly spiced with an atmosphere of danger and mystery.

Watch for HOUSE OF STORMS—coming in October!

HOFS-1